HARRY S. TRUMAN

Thirty-Third President of the United States

Illustrated by Meryl Henderson

HARRY S. TRUMAN

Thirty-Third President of the United States

by George E. Stanley

ALADDIN PAPERBACKS

New York   London   Toronto   Sydney

First Aladdin Paperbacks edition May 2004
Text copyright © 2004 by George E. Stanley
Illustrations copyright © 2004 by Meryl Henderson

ALADDIN PAPERBACKS
An imprint of Simon & Schuster Children's Publishing Division
1230 Avenue of the Americas, New York, NY 10020

Designed by Lisa Vega
The text of this book was set in Adobe Garamond.

Printed and bound in the United States of America
2 4 6 8 10 9 7 5 3 1

Library of Congress Control Number 2003096185

ISBN 978-0-689-86247-2

ILLUSTRATIONS

CONTENTS

A Son of Missouri

"Let me hold the reins, Grandpa!" four-year-old Harry Truman cried.

It was the summer of 1888, and Harry and his grandfather Young were on their way to the Cass County Fair in Belton, Missouri. They were riding in a high-wheeled cart being pulled by a strawberry roan trotting horse.

"Are you sure, Harry?" Grandpa Young said. "Nellie can be high-strung sometimes. She's used to my handling her."

Harry had watched his grandfather guide

1

the cart all over the countryside surrounding their Missouri farm. He was sure he could guide Nellie without any problems.

"Yes, Grandpa," Harry said.

Grandpa Young was a big, impressive-looking man who had strong hands and a flowing white beard. This morning, he had on his best Sunday clothes, and there was a white handkerchief tucked in the breast pocket of his coat. His beard had been neatly trimmed and combed.

"Okay," Grandpa Young said. He handed Harry the reins. "It's all yours."

Harry knew all along that his grandfather would let him drive the cart, if he asked. Harry was Grandpa Young's favorite, but Harry never took advantage of this. He loved his grandfather dearly, and he always wanted to please him.

This was one of the most exciting summers of his life, Harry had already decided. Every day for a week, he and Grandpa Young had driven the cart the six miles to the fair. Sadly for Harry, this was the last day. He'd really miss the delicious striped candy Grandpa Young always bought him. His mouth was already watering at the thought of it.

Solomon Young was one of the first settlers to arrive in Jackson County, Missouri, and was considered a very important man, so he was always asked to judge the harness races. That meant he and Harry would sit in the judges' stand, where they had the best view. Harry felt really special doing that, but he never acted special around the other kids.

Harry loved horses as much as his grandpa Young did. Grandpa Young would point out what made a good racehorse. Harry would study the horses in a particular race and, using what Grandpa Young had told him, decide which horse he wanted to bet on. The wagers were only for more pieces of striped candy, but Harry always enjoyed winning.

Harry S. Truman was born May 8, 1884, in

Lamar, Missouri, a dusty little town south of Kansas City and not too far from the road he and his grandfather were on now, but in many ways that place was like a whole different world.

The house in Lamar was tiny, compared with Grandpa Young's house. In Lamar, Harry's father, John Anderson Truman, bought and sold mules. Harry's mother, Martha Ellen—whom everybody called Mattie—took care of the household, but before she was married she attended Lexington Baptist Female College, in Lexington, Missouri, where she learned to draw, and to play the piano. It was there, too, where she learned to love literature, especially the poetry of Alexander Pope. In later life, Harry would say that it was from his mother that he learned his love of music and reading.

The mule business wasn't successful, though, so shortly after Harry was born, Mr. Truman moved his family north to a farm near Harrisonville, Missouri, where Harry's brother, John Vivian, was born. But the farm was even less successful than the mule business, so the Trumans were soon on the move again. This time it was to Grandpa Young's huge house in Blue Ridge, about sixteen miles south of Independence, Missouri.

At the moment, however, none of this was on Harry's mind. He was thinking about one horse in particular that would be racing today. It was the one he was going to bet on.

When they got to the fairgrounds, Grandpa Young hitched Nellie to a post under a shade tree, had Harry feed her some oats, and then they headed for the stables to look over the horses that would be racing today.

Along the way, Grandpa Young greeted everyone by first name. Harry always marveled at how he could do this.

"Do you know everybody in the world, Grandpa?" Harry asked.

Grandpa Young laughed and squeezed

Harry's shoulder. "No, not everyone, Harry. Many of these people came to Missouri about the same time your grandmother and I did," he told him. "We share the same history of this part of the state."

Harry thought about that. He wondered exactly what it meant to share a history with somebody.

When they reached the stables, Harry and Grandpa Young greeted all the trainers and the drivers. Their greetings were returned in a hearty manner.

As they started through the stable to look over the horses, Grandpa Young said, "Now, Harry, tell me what makes a good harness horse."

"Well, first, it's breeding," Harry began. He had committed to memory all the things that his grandfather had told him. "That means its parents were good harness racers, too."

Grandpa Young nodded.

Now, they had reached the stall of a gray

standardbred whose name was Hello My Lovely.

Harry stopped and studied the horse. He was sure this pacer would win today's race. "The horse should have wide-set eyes, a wide jaw, a big neck, a powerful chest, and straight legs and feet," he continued. "Just like this horse does."

Several people behind them started laughing. For a moment, Harry thought he had made a mistake, until one of the men said, "Well, Mr. Young, you've taught your grandson well." The man looked at Harry. "Those are powerfully big words for such a small boy."

Harry felt himself blushing, but he managed to grin at the man. "Yes, sir. I learned them from my grandpa," he said.

"Well, you just keep listening to your grandpa Young," the man said, "and one of these days you may be president of the United States."

What Harry thought then wasn't that the

man's prediction would come true, but that several members of his family had already said the same thing. Of course, he knew that many parents said that to their sons, so he didn't think any more about it.

Harry watched for a few minutes as the drivers and the trainers who had gathered around them began getting ready for the upcoming race. Suddenly, he realized that his grandpa Young had moved on to look into the other stalls, so he ran to catch up with him.

"What about this one, Harry?" Grandpa Young asked.

Harry looked at the black horse. Its name was Never Looks Back. "He's a beauty, Grandpa," he said, "but I don't think he's as good as Hello My Lovely."

Grandpa Young continued to study the horse, making Harry wonder if perhaps he had been wrong in his description of Hello My Lovely.

"His eyes are wide set and his jaw is wide,

but his neck and chest don't seem as strong as Hello My Lovely's," Harry explained. He waited for his grandfather to say something, but when he didn't, he added, "His legs and feet are straight."

"Hmm," his grandfather said as he continued to look at the black horse. Finally, he added, "I like this horse better, Harry, and I'll bet you five pieces of striped candy that it beats yours."

Harry grinned. "It's a bet," he said, shaking hands with his grandfather.

The two of them hurried out of the stable and headed for the stands. It wouldn't be long until the race began. But the closer they got to where they would be sitting, the slower Harry walked.

Finally, Grandpa Young stopped. "What's the matter, Harry?"

At first Harry didn't say anything. But when he knew his grandfather wouldn't move until he did, he said, his voice softer than usual, "I'm not sure now, Grandpa. Your horse may beat mine."

Grandpa Young raised an eyebrow and looked at Harry sternly. "Harry, why did you choose Hello My Lovely?" he asked.

Harry took a deep breath. "You've taught me all about pacers," he replied. "I think he's the best one."

"You made a decision based on what you knew to be true," Grandpa Young told him. "You can't always keep changing your mind. You have to make a decision and stick with it."

At that moment, the only thing on Harry's mind was which horse he thought would win the upcoming race, but years later, when he entered politics, Harry S. Truman would remember what Grandpa Young had told him that day. He would base all his decisions on what he knew about something. Once he had made his decision, he would stick to it.

Now walking faster, Harry followed Grandpa Young to their seats in the judges' stand.

On the track, just below him, Harry could see the drivers in their sulkies lining up. Harry had often wondered what it would be like to ride in these two-wheeled carts attached to a harnessed horse. Never Look Back and Hello My Lovely were next to each other.

"Well, Harry," Grandpa Young said. He opened his hand to reveal five pieces of striped candy. "If Hello My Lovely wins, these are yours." He grinned. "Now, what's your wager? What will you give me?"

Harry grinned back but didn't say anything.

Grandpa Young raised an eyebrow and laughed.

At that moment, a pistol sounded and the race started. Immediately, dust filled the air, and it was hard to see the horses clearly. Most harness racing tracks at fairs such as the one at Belton were small, and there was no inside running rail or fence.

In just a few minutes, though, Grandpa Young shouted, "Hello My Lovely and Never

Look Back have pulled ahead of the rest of the sulkies, Harry!"

"Come on, Hello My Lovely!" Harry shouted.

"Come on, Never Look Back!" Grandpa Young shouted.

As he always did, Grandpa Young started calling the race. "They're neck and neck as they make their way around the track, Harry."

"Come on, Hello My Lovely!" Harry shouted again.

"Now they're taking the last curve on their way to the finish line," Grandpa Young said. "Hello My Lovely has begun to pull ahead."

"Come on! Come on!" Harry shouted. "You can do it."

"Never Look Back has pulled even again," Grandpa Young said.

All of a sudden, Harry wondered if he had been wrong about his horse. Was there something about Never Look Back that he had overlooked that would let him win the race?

Then, just before they reached the finish

line, in front of Harry and Grandpa Young, Hello My Lovely pulled ahead for good.

"Hello My Lovely is the winner!" the judges shouted.

Harry took a deep breath and looked at Grandpa Young. He held out his hand.

Grandpa Young placed five pieces of striped candy in it.

"Thank you," Harry said.

With a twinkle in his eyes, Grandpa Young looked at Harry. "I'm curious, Harry," he said. "You didn't tell me what you wagered. What would you have given me if Never Look Back had won?"

Harry shrugged. "I didn't plan to lose," he said.

"I see, Harry," Grandpa Young said. "Well, you're a true son of Missouri, I can tell. You're also as stubborn as a mule!"

On the way home, Harry thought about what Grandpa Young had said. He guessed he could be as stubborn as a mule, if the occasion called for it. He understood that. But what he didn't understand was what it meant to be a true son of Missouri. He had been born in the state, he knew that. Missouri was in the heart of the United States, he also knew. Was there something about being born in Missouri that made him special? he wondered.

The rocking of the wagon and the warmth of Grandpa Young next to him began to make him sleepy. It was a pleasant feeling, and he found himself drifting off to sleep, but not before he decided that he wanted to talk to Grandpa Young some more about what it meant to be a true son of Missouri.

The Perfect Life

Two weeks after the trip to the Cass County Fair, Harry and his grandpa Young were spending a lazy Saturday afternoon together, sitting on the south porch of the big farmhouse.

"What are you thinking about, Grandpa?" Harry asked.

"About how much the bluegrass in that pasture out there looks like the bluegrass of Kentucky," Grandpa Young replied without looking at Harry. "We had a pasture with a creek running through it too."

Harry knew that both of his grandparents had come to Missouri from the state of Kentucky. He often wondered if they missed the people they knew there. For some reason, it seemed that these days Grandpa Young talked a lot about how things were when he was young. But Harry enjoyed hearing about it.

If there was one thing Harry knew for sure, though, it was that he liked living in Missouri and wouldn't want to live anywhere else.

"What were *you* thinking about, Harry?" Grandpa Young asked.

Harry shrugged. He hadn't actually been thinking about anything. He was simply enjoying sitting on the porch with his grandfather. It was hard for Harry to explain. Sometimes he didn't want to play. He just wanted to be with the members of his family and listen to them talk. He honestly didn't care what it was they talked about. He liked all their stories.

"Well, I guess you and I ought to do something more interesting than just sit here," Grandpa Young said. "Let's think about what it could be."

Just then, Harry's two-year-old brother, John Vivian, toddled out onto the porch and sat down in front of them with a thud. He gave them both a big toothless grin.

Grandpa Young shook his head in dismay. "Vivian, you're too old to be wearing your hair in curls," he said. "Why hasn't your mother cut it already? You're a boy, for goodness sakes, but you look like a girl!"

"I'm not a girl," Vivian said. "I'm a boy."

"That's what Grandpa said, Vivian," Harry said, "but it's hard for people to tell that you are."

Grandpa Young stood up. "I've made a decision, Harry. Go get Vivian's high chair and bring it out here," he said. "I'll get my shears from the barn. We're going to do something that's been needing done for a long time."

18

"You're going to cut Vivian's hair?" Harry asked incredulously.

Grandpa Young nodded. "That's exactly what I'm going to do!" he said.

"Okay, Grandpa," Harry said. He looked down at Vivian. "You stay here. We'll be right back."

As Harry entered the house, he had mixed feelings about what he and Grandpa Young were about to do. He was tired of the new kids at church asking him what his sister's name was when they'd see Vivian for the first time. Now, with short hair, Vivian would look like a boy. Of course, Harry knew how much his mother loved Vivian's curls. He was sure she wouldn't be happy when she discovered what he and Grandpa Young had done, but his mother had often told him that this was Grandpa Young's house, and in his house he made the rules. Still, Harry was sure that the rules she was talking about didn't apply to Vivian's curls.

Harry was in luck. His mother and Grandma Young were in the parlor, piecing a quilt together. No one would see him take the high chair from the kitchen.

Harry tried to pick it up and carry it, but it was heavier than he realized, so he tipped it over toward him and started dragging it out of the room. Once, it make a loud scaping sound that Harry was sure his mother and Grandma Young would hear, but after a couple of minutes, when no one had come into the kitchen to see what the noise was, he continued pulling the high chair through the rest of the house and out the screen door to the south porch.

Grandpa Young was already back from the barn when Harry arrived with the high chair. Vivian looked as if he hadn't moved an inch.

"I thought I was going to have to come get you," Grandpa Young said.

Harry positioned the high chair next to a railing and raised the tray, and Grandpa Young

20

picked up Vivian and set him on the seat.

"When I'm finished with you, Vivian," Grandpa Young said, "you'll feel more like a boy, and you'll want to do boy things."

Harry wasn't quite sure what Grandpa Young was talking about. He and Vivian were always doing *boy* things. It wasn't so much that as it was how Vivian *looked* that caused problems for Harry.

"Okay," Vivian said agreeably.

Grandpa Young took the shears and began snipping off Vivian's curls. One by one they fell onto the porch floor. It wasn't long before the curls were all gone.

"Now, then," Grandpa Young said. "You're a boy!"

"I'm a boy!" Vivian repeated.

Actually, Harry found it hard to decide exactly what Vivian really looked like now. He no longer had his curls, that was for sure, but his hair looked like it had been cut by a wheat thrasher.

"Oh!"

At the sound of his mother's voice, Harry turned to see her standing at the screen door.

"Oh!" his mother repeated.

"Mama!" Vivian said. "I'm a boy!"

Harry could see his mother's pursed lips. He noticed her heavy breathing, too. He kept waiting for her to say something, and when she finally did, it wasn't what he expected.

"Harry, I want you and Vivian to go play now. Don't worry about your chores this evening," Mrs. Truman said. She looked at Grandpa Young. "There are lots of places on the farm where two *boys* can have a lot of fun," she added.

With that, Mrs. Truman turned and headed back into the house.

Harry looked at Grandpa Young. Grandpa Young winked at him. Harry gave him a weak smile. He knew his mother was really angry about what had happened, but she hadn't said anything about it. Harry guessed that what she had told him earlier really was true: Grandpa Young was the head of the house, and when he decided to do something, that was what was done.

Harry pulled up the tray from the high chair, and Grandpa Young lifted Vivian out.

"Come on, Vivian," Harry said. "Let's take Tandy and Bob and look around the farm."

"Okay," Vivian said. He was rubbing his hands all over what was left of his hair. "I'm a boy!" he said.

Harry found Tandy, the family's black-and-white mutt, and Bob, their cat, lying within several feet of each other in the shade of the barn.

Harry dropped to his knees and began petting Tandy. Vivian, always wanting to do exactly what Harry did, started petting Bob.

"Mama's really mad about Vivian's hair, Tandy," Harry said. "I guess she doesn't want him around for a while so she won't have to look at it."

Harry lay back on his elbows and watched Vivian stroking Bob's back. Actually, Harry thought, Vivian's hair wasn't all that bad. It just took getting used to, he decided, and Harry was sure that it had been such a shock to his mother that she hadn't really looked at it carefully.

"I think I like your new haircut after all, Vivian," Harry said. "Grandpa Young did a pretty good job."

Vivian grinned and rubbed his head with one of his hands. "I'm a boy," he said.

"Yes, you are," Harry agreed. "Now, let's find something to do. It's not often Mama tells me not to do my chores."

"I want to swing," Vivian said. He stood up and started toward the swing on the old elm tree close to the house. "Come on, Harry!" he called.

"No, Vivian! We can't swing!" Harry said. "We're going to do something even more fun."

Actually, Harry wanted to swing, too, but

he knew that the swing could be seen from the room where his mother and Grandma Young were quilting, and he was sure that was a bad idea.

"What?" Vivian said.

Harry took Vivian's hand. "We're going to hunt for bird nests! Come on, Tandy!"

"Oh, boy!" Vivian said. "Come on, Bob!"

Together, the two of them started toward the trees that lined the banks of the creek. Along the way, they traipsed through prairie grass almost as tall as they were and feasted on wild strawberries.

It wasn't long before the red juice had made their hands sticky and formed red rings around their mouths.

"Look, Vivian!" Harry said. "There's a nest!"

"Where?" Vivian said.

Harry took Vivian's head in his hands and gently pointed it in the direction of a nest that was on one of the upper branches of a bush.

"Too far," Vivian said. "I want to touch."

"Uh-oh! Mama will be even more upset now," Harry said as he removed his hands from Vivian's head. "I just got strawberry juice in your hair!"

Vivian giggled.

Harry laughed too.

As they continued walking toward the creek, the trees and the bushes got thicker.

"Here's another nest, Vivian," Harry said. "But let me check it first. If birds are living in it, you can't touch it, because they won't come back to it."

At least, that's what Grandma Young had told him. Whether it was true or not, Harry didn't know, but he didn't want the birds to be without a home just because he had touched their nest.

Harry peeked into the nest. He saw several blue feathers. "I can't tell, Vivian, but why don't you just look at it this time," he said. "Maybe we'll find another one that you can touch."

"Okay, Harry," Vivian said.

A short distance farther, Harry saw a nest that had fallen from one of the trees. Inside, there were two cracked eggs and several gray feathers. Harry hoped the wind had blown it from the tree. He didn't like to think of anything worse having happened to the birds' home. He knew that sometimes bigger animals liked to eat the eggs, or even the baby birds.

"We can take this one home," Harry told Vivian. "Do you want to carry it?"

Vivian nodded.

Harry picked up the nest and handed it to his brother. "Hold it gently," he said, "or you'll ruin it."

The rest of the afternoon was spent just wandering around the farm. Harry thought it was a wonderful place to live.

Grandpa Young's farm seemed to go on and on forever. He didn't own just one farm, Harry knew, he owned *two*. The second farm was just a few miles from the one they lived on, and Harry had heard Grandpa Young say that together they were nearly one thousand acres.

"Do we have a lot of land, Grandpa?" Harry asked.

"Yes, we do," Grandpa Young said. "The Lord has been good to us, and we have to be good to the land."

Already, Harry felt something he couldn't explain. It was how close he felt to the land. All of his life, he would feel this pull. Everything about life on a farm seemed to be in perfect harmony. Harry and his family took care of the farm, and it took care of them. In the pastures there were large herds of cattle, horses, and sheep. Closer to the farmhouse, in large pens, there were hogs, chickens, ducks, and geese.

That afternoon, with Vivian in tow, gently carrying the bird's nest, Harry made a circle of the farm. From time to time, when Vivian yawned, Harry would stop so they could rest. Once, Vivian even took a nap, and it gave Harry time to think. This was his world. He couldn't imagine any other. He never wanted to leave it.

Finally, as the sun got closer to the western horizon, Harry and Vivian started back to the farmhouse.

As they neared the front porch, Vivian stopped and said, "Pony!"

Harry looked. He could see the front porch and he thought he could make out people standing in front, but he certainly didn't see a pony. What was Vivian talking about? he wondered.

"There's no pony there," Harry said.

"Yes!" Vivian insisted. "It's little. It's black."

How could Vivian see a pony and he couldn't? Harry wondered. Harry knew he often had difficulty making out the words his mother read to him from the Bible unless she used the one that she called "large print." From time to time, too, other members of the family mentioned things they saw in the distance that Harry didn't see, and he had wondered why he couldn't see whatever it was until he got closer to it. It had never occurred to him that he should say something about this to his parents.

"Hurry!" Vivian said. "I want to pet the pony."

Finally, Harry and Vivian got close enough to the front porch that Harry could indeed make out that his mother and his grandparents were standing on the porch, watching them approach, while his father stood in the yard holding the reins of a beautiful black Shetland pony!

Harry had asked his father many times if he could ride alongside him as he made his rounds on the farm, but his father always said that the horses were too big for him. This pony seemed just the right size.

"Pony! Pony!" Vivian shouted. "Come on,

Harry!" he said. With that, he started running toward the house.

Harry was right behind him.

When they reached the porch, Mr. Truman handed Harry the reins. "I need someone to help me on the farm, Harry, and I couldn't think of anyone who'd be better than you," he said. "I saw this pony in town and thought he and this saddle were just your size."

"Oh, thank you, Papa!" Harry said.

When Harry continued to just stand there, Grandpa Young said, "Get on him, Harry. Ride him around the yard."

Harry didn't need any more coaxing. He had watched his father mount his horse often enough that he knew what to do. He put his left foot in the stirrup, swung his right foot over, and was in the saddle.

"It feels good," Harry said. He made a clicking sound, gave the pony a tap on the shoulder with the reins, and started around the front yard.

After the fourth circle, Mr. Truman picked up Vivian and set him on the saddle in front of Harry. Harry made two more circles around the front yard.

Then his father said, "Well, this pony's had a long day, so I think we need to unsaddle him, feed him, and put him in his stall. We'll give him a good rubdown with some liniment and let him rest tomorrow, because you and he will have a long workday starting early Monday morning."

With Harry holding the reins with one hand and Vivian's hand with the other, they and Mr. Truman headed for the barn. Once again, Harry thought about how wonderful his life was on the farm. He didn't want or need anything else. He hoped this would last forever.

As the days passed, Mrs. Truman and Grandma Young began preparing the summer foods that would last the family through the winter months. Harry and Vivian helped pick the apples, peaches, and grapes, which were turned into jellies, jams, preserves, and butters. They gathered nuts that were used in candies and cookies. Harry could never get over how abundant the food supply was. They never went hungry.

When it got colder, he knew, after what Grandpa Young called "the first freeze," it was hog-killing time—and that meant hams, bacon, and homemade sausages, along with pickled pigs' feet, which were a favorite of Grandpa Young. Nothing was wasted, either. The fat from all of the hogs was turned into lard for frying by boiling it in a huge iron kettle. Harry's mouth watered just thinking about it all.

Summer was also a time when family came for visits, and Harry was thrilled when, one morning, his mother told him that Uncle Harry was coming that day.

Harry and Vivian both adored their mother's brother. Harry, especially, felt close to him, because they shared the same name.

All day long Harry paced the floor, frequently looking out the windows. He would have gone out to play, but his mother had already dressed him and Vivian in clean clothes.

"When's he coming?" Harry asked.

Mrs. Truman put down her embroidery needle and looked at the grandfather clock across the room. "It takes a long time to drive here from Kansas City, Harry, and I don't know for sure when your uncle started," she said. "He'll be here when he gets here, I suppose." She let out a sigh. "You and Vivian may go out onto the front porch, if you wish, but you may not go out into the yard. I want you to be presentable when Uncle Harry arrives."

Harry was glad to escape from the house. He was beginning to feel like a prisoner in some jail. Now he would probably hear his uncle's carriage coming down the road. Harry knew that he wouldn't see it until it was in the yard, and he had been thinking about that ever since Vivian had seen his black pony before he had. He had yet to mention this fact to anyone, but he had been testing himself. From time to time, he'd ask Vivian to tell him what he saw in the distance, as though it were a game, and when Vivian told him things that were only a blur to him, he began to think that something was wrong with his eyes. It scared him.

"Let's play a game, Vivian," Harry said. "Whoever sees Uncle Harry's horse and buggy first is the winner."

"Okay, Harry," Vivian said.

Just as Vivian started to get restless with having to sit so long in a chair on the porch, Harry thought he heard neighing in the distance.

"Do you see anything, Vivian?" Harry asked.

From where they were sitting on the porch, they had a good view of the road.

When Vivian looked, he said, "Yes! I see a horse! And now I see a buggy!" He turned to Harry. "Do I win?"

Harry was sure it was Uncle Harry. "I think you may have won, Vivian!" he said.

Within minutes, Harry could make out the outlines of a horse and carriage. In the distance, a voice shouted, "I see my two favorite nephews sitting on the porch!"

Yes, indeed, Harry knew now. It was Uncle Harry!

Harry wanted to run down the road and follow the buggy into the yard, but he knew that the dust from the wheels would cover his new clothes and that his mother would be really upset, so he held Vivian's hand and together they stood on the porch steps to wait for Uncle Harry.

The rest of the family had heard Uncle Harry's call, too, and had now come out to join them. Harry could feel his heart pounding. Uncle Harry was a bachelor, which

Harry knew meant he wasn't married, and he always brought a lot of gifts for everyone in the family. When he came for a visit, it was just like Christmas.

Uncle Harry pulled the horse and buggy up in front of the porch, jumped out, and tied the reins to a hitching post.

He grinned at Harry and Vivian, opened his arms wide, and said, "Give me a big hug!"

Harry and Vivian ran to him, and Uncle Harry picked them both up at once. "My goodness!" he said. "You're getting so heavy that I don't think I'll be able to do this much longer!"

That made both Harry and Vivian giggle.

Uncle Harry carried Harry and Vivian into the house, then he put them down and hugged Grandma Young and Mrs. Truman.

"I need a cup of coffee," Uncle Harry said. He turned to Harry and Vivian. "There are some packages in the buggy. Why don't you two go bring them in for me?"

Harry could only imagine what Uncle Harry had brought them from Kansas City. He and Vivian easily found the packages stored in the back of the buggy. They were wrapped in bright ribbons and colored paper. There were so many presents, in fact, that it took Harry and Vivian several trips to get them inside the house.

"For us?" Vivian asked.

Harry shook his head. "No. Uncle Harry brings presents to everybody," he said. When Vivian looked sad, Harry added, "But most of them are for us, I think."

Harry was right. He and Vivian each had three boxes. Uncle Harry always made sure that he treated them equal. One box contained a wooden horse attached to a wooden buggy. One box contained a suit, a shirt, some socks, and a pair of shoes that were for Sunday. One box contained candy and nuts.

Harry and Vivian ran over and hugged Uncle Harry's neck.

"Thank you for everything, Uncle Harry," Harry said.

"Thank you," Vivian said.

"You're both very welcome," Uncle Harry said. "You two are very special to me."

"You may change your clothes now, boys," Mrs. Truman said, "and then you may go outside and play with your toys."

Harry and Vivian hurried to their bedroom and quickly undressed, then Harry hung their clothes in the closet.

"Let's play like we're Uncle Harry, Vivian," Harry said. "We'll drive our horses and buggies from Kansas City to the farm and back."

Vivian thought that was a great idea.

They hurried out to the big old elm tree in the front yard. Harry found several rocks. He placed one rock under the tree, then he placed ten rocks several feet away.

"This one rock is our farm," he said, "and these ten rocks are the houses in Kansas City, because it's a big town."

For the next hour, Harry and Vivian drove back and forth from Kansas City to the farm.

Just as they started to get tired of so much traveling, Grandma Young appeared on the front porch. "We're all having lemonade and cookies on the porch, boys!" she called. "Would you two like some?"

"Yes, ma'am!" Harry called.

He and Vivian stood up, dusted themselves off, and headed for the porch. Now, Harry knew, he'd get to listen to Uncle Harry talk about all the things that were going on in Kansas City.

Could life be more wonderful than this? Harry wondered. He never wanted anything to change.

Harry Can't See
Very Well

Unfortunately, over the next year, Harry's life on the farm did begin to change.

He awakened one morning to find the sun streaming in his eyes—something that almost never happened to him. Since the clock was on the opposite wall, Harry couldn't see the hands. He slipped out of bed, hurried over to it, and was surprised to learn that it was eight o'clock. Harry never slept that late—even in the summer. He was always up by six o'clock, at least. There were chores to be done before breakfast, and breakfast was usually at seven o'clock. What had happened? he wondered.

Vivian was still asleep, so, not wanting to awaken his brother until he had found out what was going on, Harry slipped quietly out of the bedroom, still clad in his nightshirt. He headed for the kitchen, usually the center of activity during the morning, but when he got there, the kitchen was deserted. There were a couple of cups and plates and some silverware on the table, and the plates had pieces of leftover food on them, which was something else that was strange, because Harry's mother and Grandma Young would never leave a table like this. Dishes were done right after the meal.

Harry was scared. Just then, Mrs. Truman came into the kitchen, a teakettle in one hand and a couple of washcloths in the other. She blinked when she saw Harry. Harry could tell that she was upset about something.

It was hard for him to find the words, but

he finally managed to say, "What's wrong, Mama?"

"Oh, Harry, it's your grandpa Young," his mother said, barely able to keep her voice steady. "He's sick. He's not doing very well at all."

Harry was sure he had heard his mother incorrectly. Never in his entire life did he remember his Grandpa Young being sick. He was big and strong. How could somebody like that be sick? Harry wondered.

Mrs. Truman took a small handkerchief out of the pocket of her apron and blew her nose. "He was asking for you, Harry, so if you want, you may go see him, but if what he has is contagious, I don't want you and Vivian to catch it, so don't . . . well . . ." His mother didn't finish her sentence. Instead, she turned around to set the kettle back onto the stove. "Grandma Young needs some more hot water, so I have to boil it. You may go in now, if you're quiet."

Harry hurried down the hallway toward his grandparents' bedroom. He gently pushed the door open and was able to make out the outline of his grandfather lying in his great bed. Grandma Young was sitting in a chair beside it, wiping Grandpa Young's face with a cloth.

The door made a squeaking noise, causing his grandmother to turn around. "Come in, Harry," she whispered. "Grandpa Young has been asking for you."

Harry slipped inside the room, gently closing the door behind him. He didn't like the way the room smelled. Now, as he got closer, seeing his grandpa Young lying so still reminded him of another time and another grandfather, his grandfather Truman.

Harry had also been in the house when his Grandfather Truman died. Harry hadn't known anything was really wrong until he'd seen several relatives crying. When he found out what had happened, he immediately ran to the bedroom, where Grandfather Truman still lay, and started pulling on his beard. "Wake up, Grandpa! Wake up!" he remembered shouting.

Harry kept shouting it until his father came into the room and pulled him away. Later his father had explained to him that people get old and die. Harry knew about death, because he lived on a farm and he was always seeing dead birds and skunks and things like that. He also knew that cows and pigs died, because they were food for people to eat. But he had never thought that the people he loved would ever die.

Harry swallowed hard and walked closer to the bed. "Is Grandpa Young going to die?" he asked.

"Oh, Harry, let's not talk that way," Grandma Young whispered. She continued to sponge Grandpa Young's face with the cloth. "Your grandfather just had a spell, that's all. He seems to be breathing easier now, which

means the worst may be over. The doctor will be here this evening. Everything will be just fine, I'm sure."

Just then, Grandpa Young opened his eyes. He lifted his arm and said, "Come here, Harry."

Harry cautiously approached the bed and took hold of Grandpa Young's hand. "How are you feeling, Grandpa?" he asked.

"Don't worry about how I'm feeling, Harry. How are *you* feeling?" Grandpa Young said. "It's you I'm worried about."

Harry's mother came into the bedroom with the kettle and poured some of the steaming water into a basin sitting on the table beside the bed. "Let me do that, Mother," she said to Grandma Young. "You need to eat something."

Grandma Young stood up unsteadily, using her free hand to balance herself. "Come on, Harry," she said. "Let's get Vivian and have some breakfast."

As Harry followed his grandmother out the door, he took one last look at his grandpa

Young. *Why is Grandpa worried about me?* he wondered.

In his heart, Harry had believed his grandmother when she had said she thought the worst was over, but after breakfast he would say a prayer for his grandfather. Harry just couldn't imagine life on the farm without him.

Within another week, Grandpa Young was starting to complain about the doctor's orders to stay in bed, and a week after that he was dressed and had resumed his place at the head of the table, where he was also issuing orders to Harry's father and the rest of the household about how to run the farm.

No one complained, though, because with Grandpa Young in charge again, everything seemed right with the world.

Harry had often heard his grandma Young say that when bad things happen, they happen in threes, but he had never thought that it applied to him. Then, several days later, he was in the kitchen, eating a peach, when the pit got stuck in his throat.

"Mama! Harry!" Vivian cried. "Mama! Harry!"

Mrs. Truman turned to see what Vivian was so upset about and noticed Harry standing perfectly still except for a gagging sound coming from his throat.

"Harry!" Mrs. Truman cried. She looked at Vivian. "What was your brother doing?"

"Peach," Vivian said.

Now Mrs. Truman could see the peach juice dripping from Harry's hands onto the floor. Quickly, she grabbed Harry's back with one arm to steady him, then she stuck a finger in his mouth and pushed the pit down his throat.

Harry began gasping for air, but in a few minutes was breathing normally.

"Mama, my throat hurts," Harry managed to say.

"The pit may have scraped the inside of your throat, Harry, but it'll heal," Mrs.

Truman said. "I'll make sure everything you eat for the next few days is soft."

Just as his mother had said, after a few days, his throat no longer hurt when he ate or drank.

But now he was worried about what was going to happen to him next. Where before, his grandmother's belief that bad things come in threes had no meaning for him, now he believed that it did. What he couldn't figure out, though, was what number he was on. Should he count his grandpa Young's serious illness? he wondered. Although it wasn't Harry who was sick, Grandpa's illness certainly affected him. How many more bad things would happen?

That question was answered the next day, Sunday. Harry was already dressed for church, but he still had to comb his hair. He took pride in how he looked. Besides, he had decided, he was old enough to do this himself without having to wait for either his mother or his grandmother.

Unfortunately, the mirror he needed to use was hanging over the tall chest in his bedroom, which meant he'd have to stand in a chair to use it. There was only one chair in Harry and Vivian's bedroom, an old family heirloom that had come all the way from Kentucky. Harry liked the chair a lot. It was where his mother sat when she read to him and Vivian, and it was where she slept at night when either of them was sick.

Harry pulled the chair over in front of the chest, got his comb and brush out of one of the drawers, and climbed up onto the seat.

Perfect! he thought. Now, he could . . .

At that moment, however, Harry lost his balance and fell backward onto the hard floor. He heard a cracking noise and then felt a sharp pain just below his neck.

"Harry, we're ready to . . ." Mrs. Truman took one look at Harry lying on the floor, moaning, and cried, "Oh no, Harry! What's wrong?" She knelt down and started feeling for broken bones. "Did you hit your head?" she asked.

"No, Mama, but I hit my shoulder, and it hurts," Harry said. "It's the second or third bad thing."

"Don't try to talk, Harry," Mrs. Truman said. "It'll be all right."

She caressed his forehead with her gentle hands, and Harry immediately felt better. If anyone could make things better, it was his mother.

Mrs. Truman called Harry's father and Grandma Young into the room. Mr. Truman gently lifted Harry from the floor and placed him on his bed.

"I'm sorry, Mama," Harry said. "I just wanted to comb my hair to show you that I can do it."

"I know it was just an accident, Harry, but don't try to talk," Mrs. Truman said. "Your father will take the buggy to the doctor's and bring him back. Just be still."

While the rest of the family changed out of their Sunday church clothes, Mrs. Truman pulled the chair from in front of the chest over to the side of Harry's bed and sat with him, singing softly, caressing his forehead, and talking to him gently.

"Harry, what did you mean when you said this was either the second or third bad thing?" his mother asked.

Harry told her.

"Oh, goodness, Harry, that's just a saying," his mother told him. "I don't really think your grandma Young believes it."

"But bad things have been happening, Mama," Harry insisted.

"Bad things will happen, son, but that's just life," Mrs. Truman told him.

A few minutes later, Mr. Truman returned with the doctor, who quickly examined Harry and told the Trumans that he had broken his collarbone.

"He'll need to stay in bed, as still as possible,

for a few days," the doctor said. "I'll wrap his shoulder so that when you move him, he won't disturb the bone and keep it from healing."

With the help of Mrs. Truman, the doctor immediately went to work and, within just a few minutes, he had wound cloth around Harry's right shoulder and his neck so that movement was almost impossible. Still, Harry wasn't uncomfortable, and after a couple of days, he was even able to sit up.

Mr. Truman would carry him into the kitchen, where he could sit at the table with the rest of the family. After that, Mr. Truman would carry him onto the south porch, where he could sit and watch what was going on around him. Of course, things too far from the porch were still a blur to him, but Harry still hadn't mentioned this to anyone yet.

Harry's life with the broken collarbone took on its own routine, and he easily adjusted to it, although there were times when he wished he could wander around the farm or ride alongside his father. But Harry contented himself with just thinking about things.

Of all the people in his family, Harry had decided that it was his mama who understood him best. She was the smartest one in the family, he thought, and she seemed to care the most about him. Of course, he loved his father, but Harry never seemed to identify with him. His father was there and took care of the family financially, but there seemed to be something missing.

Harry loved it when his mother read to him from the Bible. It seemed now that she took even more time with him since he needed to spend so much time resting.

"The bread is in the oven now, Harry," his mother said, "so I thought you and I could read some from the Bible."

"Oh, good, Mama," Harry said. "First, you can read to me, and then I can read to you."

"I like that idea very much, Harry," Mrs. Truman said. "I'm a bit tired today."

Since this Bible had large print, the letters had been easy for Harry to see, so for as long as he could remember, his mother would hold him in her lap, reading all the exciting stories from the Old and New Testaments. Mrs. Truman would stop from time to time and show Harry a word. Harry would repeat it, sounding out each letter. His mother would also show him which letters had different sounds. Soon, Harry was reading some of the verses to her.

After that, it became part of their daily routine, where Mrs. Truman would read one verse and then Harry would read the next verse.

On this day, his mother let him read most of the verses. When they finally finished the chapter, Mrs. Truman said, "Harry, I have to go inside now. Do you need anything?"

"No, Mama, I'm fine," Harry said, "but are you all right?" Harry had noticed beads of perspiration on his mother's face.

"Yes, it's just warm, that's all," Mrs. Truman

said. "I'll send Vivian outside to stay with you. Please try to keep him entertained as best you can."

"All right, Mama," Harry said. "If he'll sit still long enough, I'll read him some stories from the Old Testament. They're very exciting."

"That's a good idea, Harry," his mother said. She stood up and started inside the house. "I love you very much, Harry," she said as she opened the screen door. "Always remember that." She gave him a big smile.

"I love you, too, Mama," Harry said.

A few minutes later, Vivian came outside. "Mama said you were going to tell me a story," he said. He sat down on the porch steps. "Okay, Harry, I'm ready."

"I'm not going to *tell* you a story, Vivian," Harry said, "I'm going to *read* you a story from the Bible."

Harry was halfway into the story when his father and the doctor drove up in the buggy. Harry didn't even know that his father had been gone, but then he was always busy with one project or another, working with the hands on the farm, or talking to some of the men in the surrounding towns about different ways to make money.

"How are you feeling, Harry?" the doctor asked him.

"Fine," Harry said. "I know how to read, and I'm reading a story to Vivian."

"You're a very intelligent young man," the doctor said as he gently felt Harry's collarbone. "I'm proud of you for learning to read, and I'm proud of you for taking such good care of yourself. I think we'll be able to take this sling off later today. Now, I have some other business to attend to. You go right on with your reading."

For the next hour, Harry read to Vivian about Jonah and the Whale and Noah and the Flood. When he finished, the boys played games for a while.

Harry was just about to suggest that they go

inside and ask Grandma Young for a cold glass of lemonade, when they heard a baby cry.

Harry and Vivian looked at each other. At first, Harry thought it might be a baby lamb because it sort of sounded like that, but then what would a baby lamb be doing in their house? he wondered.

Just then, Mr. Truman came out onto the porch. He had a big grin on his face.

"We heard a noise, Papa," Harry said. "It sounded like a baby crying."

"It *was* a baby crying, boys," Mr. Truman said. "That was the voice of Mary Jane Truman, your new sister!"

Harry felt his mouth drop open.

"Can we see her?" Harry managed to ask.

"Not just yet. We need to wait a while," Mr. Truman said. "The doctor is still with your mother."

At that moment, it occurred to Harry that the doctor's main reason for coming today was not really to see him, but to deliver his

60

baby sister. Suddenly afraid that a third bad thing was going to happen, he asked, "What about Mama?"

"She's just fine," Mr. Truman assured him. "She's delighted to have a daughter now."

Harry felt himself relaxing. He was positive now that all the bad things had already happened to him: his grandpa Young's illness, his swallowing the peach pit, and his breaking his collarbone. Now, he realized, he wouldn't have to worry about that anymore.

Finally, that evening, Mr. Truman took Harry and Vivian into the bedroom to see their new baby sister.

"Why did you call her Mary Jane?" Harry asked.

"That was your grandmother Truman's name," Mr. Truman said. "She died before you were born, but she was a wonderful woman, and your mother and I thought this would be a way to keep her memory alive."

Harry adored his baby sister. He was positive that whenever he looked at her, she would smile at him.

"Would you get that blue blanket for me, Harry?" Mrs. Truman asked him one day.

Harry looked around. "Where is it, Mama?" he asked.

Mr. Truman looked at him closely. "Harry, do you honestly not see where it is?"

Harry turned to his mother. "No, Mama, I don't," he said.

Suddenly, Harry was scared. Had breaking his collarbone only been the second bad thing of three? he now wondered. Was the third bad thing about to happen?

His mother named some other objects around the room and asked Harry to point them out to her. He couldn't.

"Oh, Harry, I didn't know," Mrs. Truman said. "When I can ride in the buggy, we're going to take you to Kansas City to have your eyes examined."

We're Moving to Independence!

A month later, Harry's mother felt strong enough to make the trip to Kansas City so Harry could see the eye doctor.

"Your uncle Harry has made an appointment with a friend of his, a Dr. Franks," Mrs. Truman explained. "He's supposed to be one of the best optometrists in the whole state of Missouri."

Uncle Harry had also agreed to come to the farm with his buggy to drive them to Kansas City. Mary Jane had to go with them, since Mrs. Truman was still nursing her.

Harry wondered how in the world the four of them would fit into Uncle Harry's small buggy, but on the day that Uncle Harry arrived, he was in a much larger buggy, this one pulled by *two* horses.

"It belongs to another friend of mine, and it rides really well too," Uncle Harry said. He winked at Harry. "There's nothing too good for my family!"

Harry grinned back.

Uncle Harry put their valises in the back, then helped Mrs. Truman onto the backseat, gave her a quilt for her legs, and then handed Mary Jane to her. Next, he lifted Harry onto the seat beside him. "You can help me drive," he said.

Grandpa and Grandma Young and Vivian were standing on the porch. Vivian cried and begged to go with them. Harry could tell that his mother was getting upset just watching Vivian's mournful face.

"I'll be right back," Harry said.

Without waiting for anyone to say anything, he jumped down from the buggy and ran up onto the front porch. He whispered something in Vivian's ear, kissed his cheek, then ran back to the buggy, where Uncle Harry extended a hand to help him up.

Mrs. Truman leaned forward. "How ever did you get Vivian to stop crying?" she asked Harry.

"I promised I'd bring him something from Kansas City," Harry said. "That's all."

"My goodness, I never thought of that," Mrs. Truman said. She settled in comfortably, cradling Mary Jane and singing softly to her while Uncle Harry began telling Harry all about the places in Kansas City that he was going to take them.

"Of course, we'll do this after you get your glasses, Harry," he said, "because I want to make sure you *see* all of the sights."

"I want to see them too, Uncle Harry," Harry said.

All of a sudden, Harry felt an excitement he had never felt before. The fact that he would now be able to see things that were once just a blur was almost too much to imagine.

From the moment Harry had learned that they would be going with Uncle Harry in a buggy to Kansas City, he had thought of a thousand questions he wanted to ask his favorite uncle. But with the gentle rocking of the buggy and his mother's soft singing, Harry began to get sleepy. When he finally awakened a few hours later, he was startled to see that they were on a paved street in front of a big house.

"Is this where you live, Uncle Harry?" Harry asked sleepily.

"No. I live about five miles from here, but it is on this same street," Uncle Harry said. "This house belongs to Dr. Franks."

They all got out, and Uncle Harry rang the bell.

A servant girl ushered them into a waiting

room. Soon after, a smiling Dr. Franks entered the waiting room, shook hands with Uncle Harry, and gave Mrs. Truman a slight bow. He tucked Mary Jane under the chin, then stooped down and turned his attention to Harry. "So this is the young man who thinks he needs glasses?" he said.

"Yes, sir," Harry replied.

"Well, Harry, we'll take a look and see what the problem is," Dr. Franks said. He stood up and looked at Uncle Harry. "You get to know your niece, and I'll take Harry and Mrs. Truman into the examination room."

When they got to Dr. Franks's examination room, he had Harry sit in a big chair.

"When did you first notice that Harry didn't see well?" he asked Mrs. Truman.

"Oh, Dr. Franks, I feel like such a negligent parent," Mrs. Truman began. "Now that I think about it, there have been a lot of little things that I should have paid more attention to over the years."

"Don't punish yourself, Mrs. Truman. This is not your fault," Dr. Franks said. "It's unusual for children this young to have such poor eyesight—and if they do, they usually don't know that it's bad, so they can't tell us."

"Well, I do remember thinking, this past July fourth, that Harry was reacting more to the *sound* of the fireworks at the local picnic than he was to the fireworks themselves," Mrs. Truman said. "Now I don't think he actually saw them, because they were too far away."

Dr. Franks got out a large magnifying glass and looked at Harry's eyes. "Do your eyes hurt, Harry?" he asked.

"No, sir, they don't hurt," Harry replied.

"I don't see any disease in them, so I think I can fix you up so that you can see better," Dr. Franks said. "Just sit here while I get some different pairs of glasses for you to try on. We'll see which ones fit you best."

But the glasses that Dr. Franks brought out seemed really big to Harry. The nosepieces were too wide, and the earpieces were too long. Harry wondered how in the world glasses would stay on his face.

"Those glasses seem like they're more for grown-ups," Mrs. Truman said to Dr. Franks.

Harry smiled at his mother.

"Oh, these *are* for adults, because very few children wear glasses," Dr. Franks explained. "Right now I'm only concerned with finding the right lens strength, then we'll worry about making them the right size."

"Can you see any better now, Harry?" Mrs. Truman asked.

"No," Harry said. He took off the glasses. "I can't see any better at all," he added sadly.

"Are you sure you'll be able to help him, Dr. Franks?" Mrs. Truman asked anxiously.

"Oh, yes, we've just started," Dr. Franks replied. "I'm sure Harry is going to need much thicker lenses."

Dr. Franks opened another cabinet and took out a second pair of glasses.

Harry tried them on. Once more, they were too large, but Harry said, "I can see a little better with these."

Dr. Franks nodded. He took a third pair of glasses from the cabinet, and Harry tried them on.

"Oh, this is wonderful!" Harry looked around the room. "I can see *everything* in here."

"Now that we know which lenses you need," Dr. Franks said, "I can make you a pair of wire frames."

Dr. Franks carefully measured the distance between Harry's nose and eyes and the distance from his eyes to his ears. Within just a few minutes, Dr. Franks had put together a new pair of glasses.

"Here, Harry," he said. "I think they'll be just right."

Dr. Franks gently placed the glasses on

Harry's nose and around his ears; then he stood back. "What do *you* think?" he asked.

Harry looked around the room. "They're comfortable," he said, "and I can see very well, but . . ."

"But what?" Mrs. Truman asked anxiously.

"They're so heavy," Harry replied. "Do I really have to wear glasses that are so thick?"

"I'm afraid you do, Harry. It takes a thick lens for you to see," Dr. Franks replied. "And you'll have to wear them for the rest of your life."

"You'll get used to wearing them, Harry, I'm sure," Mrs. Truman said. "It'll just take a little time."

"That's right," Dr. Franks agreed, "but you'll have to be careful not to break them, so you'll need to make sure that you don't play rough with your friends."

"I won't," Harry promised.

Mrs. Truman paid Dr. Franks his fee; then they left the examination room.

On the drive to Uncle Harry's house, Harry

was absolutely amazed at the things he could see. He decided right then that whatever he *couldn't* do because he now wore glasses was outweighed by what he could see. He knew that he would never complain about it.

When Harry and his family returned to Grandpa Young's farm, Harry felt as though he were starting a new life. He had no idea how many things he had been unable to see before, and was amazed to discover all the things that had always been on the farm but were new to him.

Grandpa Young had always pampered Harry and Vivian, letting them do almost anything they wanted to do on the farm, and after Harry got his glasses, his mother did the same, but that soon ended one warm spring day in 1890.

Harry and Vivian were playing on the front porch when they heard a wagon coming toward the house. They raced to see who it was.

"Papa!" the boys cried.

Mr. Truman had just returned from the nearby town of Grandview, where he had been for almost a week on business.

Mr. Truman hugged both the boys and said, "I've got a surprise for you!" He reached into the buggy and pulled out a little red wagon.

"Oh, thank you, Papa!" Harry said. He turned to Vivian. "I'll take you for a ride, okay?"

Gleefully, Vivian got into the wagon, and Harry started pulling him around the yard.

"Watch out for the puddles," Mr. Truman called to them.

"Okay, Papa!" Harry called back.

Harry pulled Vivian around and around—and even Tandy and Bob jumped into the wagon for a ride.

Harry was on his fourth circle around the house when a horse and buggy belonging to a neighbor drove into the yard.

"It's Mrs. Jones and Edward," Harry said.

He and Vivian ran to greet them. Harry tied the reins to the hitching post.

"I've come to help your mother with some sewing," Mrs. Jones said. "Edward wanted to come along."

"Look, Edward," Vivian said. "Papa brought us a new red wagon."

"I like it," Edward said. "May I ride in it too?"

"Sure. I can pull both of you," Harry said. "Tandy and Bob were riding in it with Vivian before you got here."

Edward climbed into the wagon, and Harry started pulling them around the house.

Soon, though, Harry was getting bored of making circles around the house, so he said, "This train is going someplace else." He opened a gate to the pasture. "We're going to Kansas City!" Harry still remembered when Uncle Harry had taken them to Kansas City's Union Station so they could watch all of the trains coming and going. What Harry wanted more than anything now was to go on a long train ride. If he couldn't do it for real just yet, he could pretend that the red wagon was a train and that Edward and Vivian were the passengers.

"Yay! Kansas City!" Vivian said. "We can see Uncle Harry!"

"I can't go there," Edward said, sounding a little anxious. "Mama said I had to stay close enough that she could call me."

"Oh, we're not really going to Kansas City," Harry explained. "We're just going to pretend that the barn is Kansas City."

But halfway to the barn, under a big maple tree, Harry decided to rest in the shade. The trip to the barn was longer and harder than he had thought it would be.

"This train is stopping here so we can eat," Harry said.

Vivian and Edward got out of the wagon, and the three of them lay under the shade of the maple tree.

"Well, it's time for the train to leave," Harry said after a few minutes. He stood up. "All aboard!"

"I don't want to play train," Edward said. "I want to play cowboys and Indians."

Vivian turned to Harry. "Me too!"

"Okay," Harry said. "We'll pretend that we're in a covered wagon on the Oregon Trail, and Tandy and Bob will be the Indians who are attacking us," Harry said. "I'll drive the wagon, and Vivian, you and Edward will ride, and when you see Tandy and Bob, you start shouting, 'Indians! Indians!'"

Vivian and Edward thought that was a great idea. They climbed into the wagon, and Harry started pulling them as fast as he could toward the barn. When Tandy and Bob saw them, they started chasing them.

"Indians! Indians!" Vivian and Edward shouted. "Here they come! Here they come!"

Harry started pulling the wagon faster, but right before he reached the barn, he ran right into a puddle, which upset the wagon and dumped Vivian and Edward into the mud.

Vivian and Edward crawled out of the puddle and onto the grass. Their clothes were soaked with the muddy water. They looked at themselves and started giggling.

"That was fun, Harry," Edward said.

"Do it again!" Vivian begged.

Edward and Vivian got back in, and Harry grabbed the handle and started running toward the puddle. Just as he reached the edge, he swerved the wagon so he'd avoid stepping into the puddle himself, and the wagon tilted, dumping Edward and Vivian into the muddy water again.

This time, Vivian and Edward started giggling right away. As they crawled out of the muddy water, soaked even more, Edward said, "Let us pull you, Harry! It's fun!"

Harry agreed, but he planned to trick them. He was sure that he'd be able to jump out of the wagon right before it reached the

puddle and escape, but Edward and Vivian turned the wagon a different way, and Harry fell into the muddy water.

Harry wasn't about to give up. He was going to show Vivian and Edward that he could outsmart them, so he asked them to do it again, but once again, he fell into the puddle before he could escape from the wagon.

All of a sudden they heard Mrs. Truman and Mrs. Jones calling them.

Harry's heart leaped to his throat. He looked at Vivian's and Edward's clothes and then he looked down at his own, and all of a sudden it wasn't funny anymore.

"Let's show Mama what we can do, Harry," Vivian suggested.

Harry shook his head. "I don't think she's going to be too happy about this," he said.

Just then, Mrs. Truman and Mrs. Jones came around the corner of the barn and stopped dead still.

"Edward!" Mrs. Jones cried. Her hand

went to her mouth. "Oh, my goodness!"

"Harry S. Truman! I'm ashamed of you!" Mrs. Truman shouted. "You boys are filthy!"

Without waiting for an explanation, Mrs. Truman broke off a branch from a nearby maple tree and stripped it of the leaves and twigs to make a long switch.

"Harry, get that wagon out of the mud this instant," she said angrily, "and pull it back to the house!"

Slowly, Harry pulled the wagon out of the mud. He couldn't imagine why he had thought this was fun in the first place. He was soaked with muddy water. He had specks of mud on his glasses, making it hard for him to see. But what he felt the worst about was that he had disappointed his mother. She always counted on him to do what was right, and today he hadn't.

As they all headed slowly back toward the house, no one said a word, but Vivian and

Edward occasionally let out little sobs.

As they walked, Mrs. Truman whipped Harry across his legs with the long switch. It stung, but Harry just winced and didn't say anything. Finally, though, he turned to his mother. "It was an accident, Mama," he said. "I didn't see the puddle, and I just ran into it."

"Well, you must have missed seeing it several times, then," Mrs. Jones said indignantly, "from the amount of mud that's on Edward's new clothes."

Harry hung his head and continued pulling the wagon toward the farmhouse.

"I don't want to hear any explanation from you, Harry," Mrs. Truman told him. "Vivian and Edward are younger and don't always have the ability to make proper judgments like you do."

"I'm sorry, Mama," Harry mumbled.

"You're supposed to keep them out of

trouble, Harry," Mrs. Truman added. "You're not supposed to get them into trouble."

Not even Harry could account for his lapse in judgment. He knew his mother expected a lot from him because he was the oldest, and he vowed never to disappoint her again.

Harry kept his promise to his mother, but his father was a different matter. Harry was never prepared for his father's outbursts. They seemed to come out of nowhere. Although Harry's father never laid a hand on him, his scoldings seemed almost worse at times. Harry had often thought that a switching would hurt less than his father's angry words.

A few weeks after Harry had gotten into trouble because of the mud puddle, Mr. Truman asked him if he'd like to ride with him while he checked the fences around the farm for broken barbed wire. Harry loved to ride his Shetland pony, so he eagerly agreed.

Together they rode to the pasture. Harry watched constantly for broken posts and barbed wire. Finding no problems, Mr. Truman suggested they check out the cattle in the pasture to see if any of them had been injured or were ill.

Harry always liked to feel that he was doing his part to help on the farm. But in trying to see if something might be wrong with a calf that was lying near the barbed-wire fence, Harry leaned too far over and fell off his pony.

He wasn't hurt, but when he stood up and looked at his father, he knew that something was wrong. Mr. Truman's face was red with anger.

"A boy who cannot stay on a pony has no business riding one, Harry!" Mr. Truman said. "You'll walk home from here."

Mr. Truman grabbed the pony's reins and started leading him back to the barn.

Harry was devastated. He didn't know

what to say. There was no way he could stop the tears, and he cried all the way back to the house.

Later, in his room, he could hear his mother and father arguing.

"You treated Harry unjustly," Mrs. Truman told him. "You had no right to do that."

Harry hardly slept that night. He didn't like being the reason his parents were angry at each other.

The next morning, however, everything seemed to have been forgotten, because when Harry went in to breakfast, everyone at the table was smiling.

"I have an announcement to make," Mr. Truman said. "We're moving to Independence."

Harry gasped. He didn't know what to say. He couldn't imagine not living on Grandpa Young's farm, but Harry knew that Independence was just a few miles from Kansas City, and he had never forgotten the wonderful sights Uncle Harry had shown them when Harry got his glasses.

"I want Harry to have the proper schooling," Mrs. Truman said. "He's a very intelligent young man, and he needs more than country schools can give him."

Harry had such a big lump in his throat that he couldn't talk, but he managed to say, "After breakfast, I'll start packing my belongings."

Diphtheria!

Even though Independence was a town, to Harry the house on South Crysler Street was like living on a small farm. There was a barn and enough land around it for his mother to have a big garden, just like the one at Grandpa Young's house, and for his father to keep several farm animals. Mr. Truman even allowed Harry to bring his black Shetland pony.

Later, he bought Harry and Vivian a pair of goats that they could harness to a cart. The boys had so much fun, they finally convinced their mother that Mary Jane would enjoy it too.

When Harry and Vivian had the two goats hitched to the cart, they set Mary Jane inside and climbed into the cart with her. Then they rode all around the yard.

Mary Jane giggled so much, she got the hiccups, and that made Harry and Vivian laugh even harder.

When Harry thought the goats needed a rest, he pulled up to the back porch and picked up Mary Jane. "I'll take her inside, Vivian," Harry said. "Why don't you take the goats to the barn and unharness them?"

"Okay, Harry," Vivian said.

Harry could have done it faster and more easily than Vivian, but he knew how important it was to Vivian to help with the farmwork.

Just then, Mrs. Truman appeared at the

back door. "Well, from all that giggling I heard, I'd say that your sister has found a new interest," she said. "You need to be prepared to do this again."

"Oh, I'll be glad to, Mama," Harry said. "I love taking care of Mary Jane."

Harry was telling the truth. He absolutely adored his little sister.

With the move to Independence, Harry found himself not having to do as many chores as he had done on Grandpa Young's farm, so he began to read more. Although there were newspapers and the occasional magazine around the house, Harry mostly read from the Bible. He never tired of rereading the passages his mother had read to him on the farm. If he couldn't remember some of the words, his mother was always there to help him.

"Now that we're living in town, it'll be easier for us to attend church regularly," Mrs.

Truman announced one Saturday night, "so I've decided that we're going to start tomorrow morning."

"How far is the Baptist Church from here, Mama?" Harry asked.

"We're not going to the Baptist Church, Harry," Mrs. Truman said. "We're going to the First Presbyterian Church."

"I thought we were Baptists," Vivian said.

"We are, Vivian, but the First Presbyterian Church is only a few blocks from our house," Mrs. Truman said, "and I think we'll be much more likely to attend every Sunday if we go to a church that's not so far away."

When Sunday morning arrived, though, Harry didn't want to get out of bed. One of the things he still wasn't used to, now that they lived in town, was how many more people he saw every day. He'd seen more people in the few months that his family had lived in Independence than he had in his whole life. Of course, Harry didn't mind *seeing* the people, he just didn't want to have to talk to them. He was afraid that he couldn't think of anything to say—at least anything that town people would be interested in.

Finally, when it seemed like his mother was getting angry, Harry got out of bed and put on his best clothes. Mr. Truman was away on business again, so Harry, Vivian, Mary Jane, and Mrs. Truman walked the three blocks to the First Presbyterian Church.

Much to Harry's delight, the Truman family was welcomed by everyone, and Harry immediately felt right at home.

A women who reminded Harry of Grandma Young took Mary Jane to the nursery.

A man who had one of the biggest smiles he had ever seen then took his mother to the class for women, where he introduced her to the teacher. Then he took Harry and Vivian to their class, where they joined other boys and girls their age on wooden benches.

"I'm glad we came, aren't you, Harry?" Vivian whispered.

Harry nodded. It hadn't been a bad experience after all. He would remember that the next time he was nervous about meeting people.

A boy next to Harry handed him a hymnal and pointed to the song that everyone had just started singing. "Amazing Grace." Harry knew this song by heart. His family had been singing it for a long time. Harry pointed out the words to Vivian and whispered, "'Amazing Grace.' You know that."

Vivian nodded.

Together they sang the hymn with the rest of the Sunday school class. Just as they reached the last verse, Harry noticed a girl who was standing across the aisle from him. She had the most beautiful golden curls that he had ever seen.

When the singing was over, the teacher offered a prayer, and then she said, "We have two new visitors this morning, boys and girls. Harry and Vivian Truman. The Truman family has just moved here to Independence. We want to welcome them."

One by one, everybody in the class stepped up to Harry and Vivian and introduced themselves.

At first, Harry forgot all about how comfortable and happy he'd thought he would be in this church. Now, he just wanted to run and hide, but after a while, he realized that some of the other boys and girls were as nervous about meeting him as he was about meeting them, so he relaxed and started to feel better.

"How do you do? I'm pleased to meet you," he said in as strong a voice as he could muster.

Finally, the girl with the golden curls stepped up. Harry saw that she also had beautiful blue eyes. "My name is Elizabeth Virginia Wallace," she said, giving him a big smile, "but everyone calls me Bess."

Harry couldn't speak. He could only stare at this girl. Finally, he managed a smile, and Elizabeth Virginia Wallace smiled back.

Most of the rest of the morning was a blur. All Harry could think about was the girl with the golden curls and the bright blue eyes. He shuddered to think that he had tried to talk his mother out of coming to this church. Now he could hardly wait for the next Sunday to come around.

For the first two years after the Trumans moved to Independence, Mrs. Truman taught Harry at home, just as she had on the farm. Harry had already learned to read and write well under her direction. Now, with his glasses, he could easily see the print in books and newspapers.

But when Harry turned eight, in 1892, Mrs. Truman decided to send him to Noland School, close to their house, so he could study with the other boys and girls in Independence. Of course, she knew that because he had never gone to a formal school, he would have to start in the first grade, but Mrs. Truman was quite sure that he would advance rapidly. After all, she assured Harry, he could already read and write.

On the morning that Harry was to start, he told his mother that he would walk to school by himself.

"They may put me in the first grade, Mama," he said, "but I want to show them I can already do a lot of things by myself."

"That's fine, Harry," Mrs. Truman said.

As Harry walked along the street toward the school, he wondered what the teacher and the other pupils would be like. His wonderful experience at the First Presbyterian Church had made him less shy about meeting new people. That, combined with the fact that he was eager to learn as much as he could, made him look forward to this experience more than ever.

When Harry reached Noland School, he went inside and looked around. He had no idea where to go. Then he saw another boy standing in the hall, so he went over to him. "I'm looking for my class," Harry said. "Can you tell me where the first grade is?"

"How old are you?" the boy asked.

"Eight," Harry replied.

"You'll be in the third grade with me," the boy said. "My name is William Jenkins."

Harry shook hands with the boy, but he said, "I've never been to a formal school before, so I'll probably need to start at the beginning, but I can already read and write, so I'll catch up pretty fast, I think, and then I'll be in your class."

William just looked at Harry for a minute, then shrugged and said, "Well, okay, I'll show you where the first grade is, then."

When they reached the first-grade room, Harry thanked William and went inside.

The teacher looked up and smiled. "Good

morning," she said. Harry was glad that she didn't say anything like, "Are you sure you're not in the wrong room?"

The teacher pointed to a desk on the side of the room by the windows. "Here is a seat for you," she said, and smiled at Harry again.

Just then, a loud bell rang outside in the hall, and the rest of the pupils hurried to their desks.

When everyone was seated, the teacher said, "Boys and girls, I'm Miss Ewing, and I'm looking forward to being your teacher this year." She looked around the room. "I think the first thing we should do is get acquainted. Since we'll all be spending the next year together, we should know one another's names, don't you think?"

"Yes, ma'am," the class said in unison.

Miss Ewing held up a book. "When you give me your name, I'll spell it out and then I'll write it down in this book. It's called a grade book. This is where I enter your grades and whether you're present or absent."

One by one, the pupils in the class stood up and gave their names to Miss Ewing. When it was Harry's turn, he stood up and said in a clear, strong voice, "Harry S. Truman, ma'am."

Miss Ewing spelled out H-A-R-R-Y, then she looked up at Harry and said, "What does the S stand for? I'll need your full middle name for the school records."

"It doesn't really stand for anything. It's just a capital S with a period after it," Harry explained.

Miss Ewing looked puzzled. "I've never heard of anyone just having an initial for a middle name, Harry," she said. "Are you sure it doesn't stand for *something*?"

"I'm positive, Miss Ewing," Harry said pleasantly. "When I was born, my father wanted to name me Shippe, after my Grandfather Truman, and my mother wanted to name me Solomon, after my Grandfather Young, so they just decided to name me S and then let people think what they wanted to."

"Well, that is interesting," Miss Ewing said. "I'll just write down S as your middle name and put a period after it."

The rest of the day went so well that, when it was time for school to be over, Harry really didn't want to leave.

As his mother had predicted, because he applied himself, he quickly passed the rest of the pupils in the class in his studies.

Unfortunately, that wasn't the case at recess. He joined in activities that didn't require a lot of running around, but his glasses kept him from participating in most of the games that everyone played. During those times, Harry would stand by the building and watch. He never minded this, and never felt as though he were missing out on anything.

One afternoon, Miss Ewing saw him and came over to where he was standing. "I wish you could be out there playing with the other children, Harry," she said.

"It's all right, Miss Ewing, really. I don't mind it at all," Harry said. "I enjoy just watching them."

The next day, Harry was watching a baseball game when he noticed that the boy who always umpired wasn't there. That gave him an idea. He walked over to the players and said, "I can be the umpire today."

"Well, we do need an umpire, but you've never played the game with us, Harry," one of the players said. "Are you sure you know the rules?"

"You're right, I've never played, but I've been watching you for a long time, and I think I do know," Harry told them. "But if I don't umpire to suit you, then just tell me and I'll go back to watching."

"It's a deal!" the players said.

Harry soon proved that he knew almost as much about baseball as the players did, and everyone on the team told him how pleased they were with his calls.

Later, Miss Ewing told Harry that she had been watching through one of the classroom windows the games he had umpired.

"I'm so proud of you, Harry S. Truman," she said. "You are a very responsible young man."

The year 1892 was not only the year Harry started at Noland School, it was also a presidential election year. There were always a lot of political discussions in the Truman household, and Harry began to take an interest in them.

Benjamin Harrison, a Republican, was running for reelection against Grover Cleveland, a Democrat. Harry's father was a strong Democrat, so he told all of his friends to vote for Cleveland. Harry began to get as excited about the election as his father was. He read every newspaper article he could find about both candidates.

When election day arrived, Mr. Truman

voted as soon as the polls opened. Afterward, he went around Independence making sure that everyone he knew voted for Grover Cleveland. Since women couldn't vote, Mrs. Truman stayed home and did her morning chores as usual.

When Harry started for school the next morning, nobody knew who had won the election, because it took a while for the votes to be counted by hand and for the information to get to people all over the United States. Finally, three days later, all the votes had been counted, and Grover Cleveland had been elected President.

When Harry got home that evening, his father had wrapped colored cloth around the pillars on the front porch and was in the process of putting up an American flag.

"What's happening, Papa?" Harry asked.

"We Democrats are going to celebrate Grover Cleveland's victory," Mr. Truman said proudly. "Tonight there will be one of the biggest torchlight parades that Independence has ever seen."

"May I stay up and watch it, Papa?" Harry asked.

"Of course you may, son," Mr. Truman replied. "Our whole family is going."

Harry would never forget that night. People jammed the streets of Independence, singing and shouting the praises of President Grover Cleveland. Harry had started to get sleepy before the parade started, and Vivian and Mary Jane had already fallen asleep, but when Harry heard the band coming down the street, he was immediately wide awake. Several wagons carrying men whom Mr. Truman called local politicians followed the band. Then came horses draped in red, white, and blue cloth. Finally, behind the horses, the people who had been lining the streets joined in, some carrying torchlights. Harry and his family joined in too, with Mr. Truman holding his torch up high. At that moment, Harry decided to learn as much as possible about politics.

But not everything that happened to Harry in 1892 was wonderful. His Grandpa Young died. Harry found it almost impossible to think that this tremendous man, who had been so much a part of his childhood, was now gone.

One year later, in 1893, Grandpa Young's farmhouse burned to the ground when a servant girl trying to light a coal-oil lamp accidently set it on fire. Almost everything was lost. A smaller house was built where the old house had been, but to Harry, life there was never the same again, and even though he never mentioned it to his parents, he didn't like going there anymore. After Grandpa Young's death, Uncle Harry moved back to live with Grandma Young so he could help with the farm—another unhappy event for Harry. Until then, his Uncle Harry would often drive over to Independence from his house in Kansas City, visits that Harry and the rest of the family looked forward to.

When school resumed in the fall of 1893, Harry continued to impress everyone with his intelligence and his hard work. He was the star pupil in Miss Minnie Ward's second-grade class.

Early in February, 1894, though, Harry's studies came to a complete halt.

One morning, Harry awakened and knew right away that he didn't feel right. But he did not want to stay home from school—he was learning faster than anyone ever thought he could, and he was very proud of that. Slowly, he got out of bed, dressed, and went downstairs to the kitchen.

After he had sat staring at his plate for several minutes without touching any of the food, his mother said, "If you don't eat something, Harry, you'll have to stay at home today, because you're not going to school on an empty stomach."

Harry gradually started picking at his food. He had to force down every bite, and several times he thought he might have to ask to be excused because he didn't know if he could keep the food down. Finally he managed to eat everything on his plate.

It was even more of a struggle to get dressed. Because it was bitterly cold outside, Harry wore several layers of clothes, but as he trudged along the street, he couldn't keep from shivering. He could hardly wait to get to school so he could warm up.

Harry managed to make it through his morning lessons, but right before lunchtime, his body ached so much he couldn't even think. All he wanted to do was go to sleep.

In the middle of the afternoon, Miss Ward walked back to his desk. "There's something wrong, Harry," she said, her voice full of concern. "I'm sending you home, but I'll write a note to your mother explaining why, so she won't think that you got into trouble."

As bad as he felt, Harry was able to grin at Miss Ward's joke. There wasn't anybody in the school who thought that Harry S. Truman would ever do anything to get himself in trouble.

Once again, Harry bundled up against the cold and left the school building. For some reason, the snow seemed even deeper. It was almost impossible to drag one foot in front of the other.

When Harry finally got home, his mother took one look at him and said, "Oh, Harry! I've been worried all day. I knew something was wrong this morning. I should have kept you home."

Mrs. Truman quickly helped Harry undress, put him to bed, and covered him up with extra blankets. Mr. Truman was in a nearby shed, repairing a harness, so Mrs. Truman went to the back door and rang a handbell to let him know that he was needed right away.

Mr. Truman came running up to the back porch. "What's wrong, Mattie?" he asked.

"It's Harry, John. He's come home sick from school," Mrs. Truman said. "You need to get Dr. Twyman right away. Harry's burning up with a fever."

"One of the horses is already saddled," Mr. Truman said.

Mrs. Truman hurried back to Harry's room. Now he was shivering uncontrollably. Mrs. Truman kept bathing his face and arms with a cold cloth until Dr. Twyman finally arrived.

Dr. Twyman examined Harry carefully. When he finished, he turned to Mr. and Mrs. Truman. "His temperature is quite elevated, and his throat is raw," he said. "There's been an outbreak of diphtheria in Independence, and I'm afraid that's what Harry has."

"Oh, my goodness!" Mrs. Truman exclaimed.

108

She turned to Mr. Truman. "I want you to take Vivian and Mary Jane to Grandma Young's, John," she said. "If they're out of the house, it might keep them from getting this horrid disease."

"That might be the best thing for Mary Jane," Dr. Twyman said, "but I'm not sure about Vivian."

"What do you mean?" Mrs. Truman asked.

"Well, if Vivian has been sleeping in the same room as Harry, he's probably already been exposed, and the disease might just be in the incubation period," Dr. Twyman explained. "If that is indeed the case, then Vivian could infect everyone at your mother's house."

Mrs. Truman closed her eyes and shook her head sadly. "Whatever you think is best, Dr. Twyman," she said.

As it turned out, Dr. Twyman was correct. Four days later, Vivian also had diphtheria.

As she always did when her children were

sick, Mrs. Truman sat by their bedside, fanning them and wiping their foreheads with cold cloths to try to break the fever.

Mr. Truman brought her meals to her, but Mrs. Truman had lost almost all interest in food.

"You're going to get sick too, Mattie, if you don't eat," Mr. Truman told her.

But Mrs. Truman still refused to eat.

Gradually, Vivian began to get better, and soon his recovery was almost complete.

But Harry developed complications and had to remain in bed. One morning, Mrs. Truman discovered that Harry was paralyzed. He couldn't speak, and he couldn't move his arms or legs. Mr. Truman rushed to get Dr. Twyman, who came right away.

"Unfortunately, this is not unusual," Dr. Twyman told them. "It is sometimes a side effect of the diphtheria."

Harry was the one who seemed the least affected emotionally by what was happening to him. He was alert and could hear very well. Since it was difficult for him to swallow, though, he could only drink and not eat.

Mrs. Truman read to him for hours at a time.

Then, after several weeks, he started getting better. Gradually, he regained the use of his muscles, and was soon able to speak and move about.

But he had been sick so long that his school had closed for the summer. That was what upset Harry the most.

"I've missed the rest of second grade," he said. "I'll never get through school if things like this keep happening to me!"

"When you're a little stronger, I'll start teaching you at home again," Mrs. Truman told him, "and then when you're able, we'll see about getting you into a summer school program."

Harry's spirits were buoyed by his mother's promise. Almost miraculously, his strength soon returned to where he was able to sit up in bed while his mother read to him in the subjects he would have studied in the last half of the second grade.

Before long, Harry was able to sit at the kitchen table and read on his own. He read everything he could get his hands on. Since the Truman household was full of books, it was always easy to find something that Harry was interested in at the moment. He especially liked reading about the careers of great generals. Robert E. Lee and Andrew Jackson were among his favorites.

The Waldo Avenue Gang

That same year, Mrs. Truman enrolled Harry in the summer school program at the Columbian School. Noland School, where Harry had attended the first and second grades, was on South Liberty Street, a long walk from his house, but the new eight-room Columbian School had just opened on South River Boulevard, and Harry had to walk only three blocks.

Harry had been at the school for just a week when his teacher, Miss Jennie Clements, said, "You're already ahead of your class, Harry, so you don't really have to do any makeup work."

Hearing that, Harry was almost disappointed, and it must have shown on his face, because Miss Clements said, "But since you're here, let's do some advanced work so that when school starts again in September, you can join a higher class."

Harry couldn't believe what he was hearing. "Do you mean that if I study really hard this summer, I can be with pupils my own age?"

Miss Clements smiled. "That's exactly what I mean," she said.

Although Harry could never say that he was glad he had been sick with diphtheria, he now realized that there is always something positive in everything that happens to a person. Miss Clements loaned Harry some of the books he would need to study, and Mr. and Mrs. Truman bought the rest. For the remainder of the summer, Harry studied day and night. He usually had to be called several times to come to meals. He never wanted to go to bed until he had finished "one more chapter." During this time, neither Mr. Truman nor Mrs. Truman scolded him once. They were almost as happy as he was with his progress against such odds.

Right before school was to resume in September, Miss Clements gave Harry an oral and a written exam on each of his subjects. He passed all of them with high marks.

"Congratulations, Harry," Miss Clements said. "You are now in the fourth grade."

When classes began that autumn at the Columbian School, Harry was with pupils his own age for the first time. Most of them would stay together through high school. One of Harry's classmates was Bess Wallace, whom he had met at Sunday school right after his parents had moved to Independence. He had never forgotten the girl with the golden curls and the bright blue eyes. He couldn't believe his good fortune to be in the same class with her.

* * * *

Harry's good fortune continued. In the spring, the Trumans moved to a new house on Waldo Avenue. This house was much like their former one, in that it had a barn and plenty of surrounding land for a garden and some farm animals—including the black Shetland pony and the pair of goats.

But what appealed to Harry and Vivian the most about the new neighborhood was that there were now plenty of people their own ages to play with.

In fact, the Trumans had hardly settled in, when some of the boys and girls in the neighborhood descended on their house, including Paul Bryant, Fielding Houchens, Elmer Twyman, Tasker Taylor, Charlie Ross, Cellie Lowe, and Ara Brown. The next day, Harry had a really big surprise. He had no idea that Bess Wallace lived nearby, so he was totally taken aback when she and her brother Frank showed up. Harry was usually

tongue-tied in Bess's presence, but he managed to welcome both of them to his house.

Having so many friends to play with was a
new experience for Harry and Vivian, and
they enjoyed it immensely. Harry let everyone ride his pony, and Vivian kept busy giving
everyone rides in the goat cart. At other
times, they all played games together.

Soon, they began calling themselves the
Waldo Avenue Gang. Since Harry was the oldest member, he became the leader. Whenever
arguments broke out, Harry always settled
them to everyone's liking.

Harry's mother let him know how pleased
she was that everyone in the neighborhood
enjoyed coming to their house. One morning, she asked him if the Waldo Avenue Gang
would be getting together today, and when
Harry said yes, Mrs. Truman told him that
she had a special surprise for them.

As usual, it wasn't long until most of Harry's

and Vivian's friends were chasing one another around the house or being pulled in the goat cart.

Mrs. Truman stepped out onto the back porch and rang a bell. Since no other mother did anything like that, it got everyone's attention, and soon every member of the gang was standing in the yard, waiting to see what was wrong.

"I think it's time for a snack," Mrs. Truman announced. "I made some fresh cookies and lemonade for you."

A cheer went up from everyone.

Mrs. Truman led the gang into the kitchen, where she had set out the cookies and glasses of lemonade.

When everyone had helped himself or herself, they all went back outside and sat down in the shade of a big oak tree.

"Your mother is a wonderful cook," Bess said. "These oatmeal-raisin cookies are delicious."

Harry smiled at her. "Thank you," he managed to say. "I like them too."

Bess returned Harry's smile.

Harry tried to think of something else to say to Bess, but nothing that made sense came to him. There was an awkward silence between them until Bess's brother Frank finally said, "Well, what are we going to do now?"

"Let's play pigtail baseball," Harry suggested. "I read about it last week in a book. It sounded kind of interesting."

"I've never heard of it," Frank said. "How do you play it?"

Harry explained the game, a version of baseball where players change positions based on how well they play.

Everyone agreed that it sounded like a lot of fun since it would include the entire Waldo Avenue Gang. Harry chose Frank as the first batter, Paul as the first catcher, and Vivian as the first pitcher. He named Bess the first shortstop. Fielding, Elmer, and Tasker covered the outfield, and Charlie, Cellie, and Ara covered the bases.

Harry agreed to act as umpire. No one in the group had ever said anything about Harry's standing on the sidelines when the rest of them played games. They just sort of looked to him as the person in charge of what they did.

Vivian wound up and threw the first pitch across the plate to Paul. Frank swung at it and missed.

"Strike!" Harry shouted.

Vivian threw the second pitch, and this time Frank hit the ball into center field. It dropped in front of Elmer, but he quickly picked it up and, seeing Frank running toward second, threw it to Cellie. Cellie caught the ball, but Frank had already touched the base.

"Safe!" Harry shouted.

Since Frank was still on base, everyone had to move up a position so there would be a batter, so that meant that Paul was next. He hit a ball directly to Bess, who was now at second. She tagged Frank while he was trying to reach third and then threw the ball to first, putting out Paul.

Harry couldn't believe his eyes. Bess Wallace was not only the most beautiful girl he knew, she was also the best baseball player. He had never known anyone so perfect!

That night, Harry lay in bed thinking about his life—not just what had happened already, but what would take place in the future. Where would he go, if anywhere, beyond Independence, he wondered, and what would he be? He could still remember how he had felt when he'd lived on Grandpa Young's farm. At the time, he was sure that that would always be his home. He knew now that things never happened the way you thought they would.

Beyond the Trumans' back fence, about 150 yards away, was the Missouri Pacific depot. On the north side of the house were the line's main tracks, which were so close that when the trains went by—and they came in both directions almost hourly—the dishes in the kitchen rattled. Mrs. Truman didn't like it one bit, but she tolerated it, and the rest of the family didn't seem to care one way or the other. But to Harry, trains were an endless fascination. As each one passed, Harry imagined himself on the train.

Just then, the eastbound *Kansas-Nebraska Limited* shrieked by on its way to St. Louis.

One of these days, I will go lots of places on trains, Harry decided as he finally closed his eyes. *I'm sure of it.*

A Bad Accident

"Harry!"

Harry looked up from the woodpile, where he had been splitting chunks of wood into sticks for the stove. Caroline Simpson, the family's black cook—whom Harry and Vivian sometimes called Aunt Caroline—was standing at the back door, hands on her hips. "Yes, Aunt Caroline? What's the matter?"

"I need some of that wood you've been chopping out there," Aunt Caroline said. "I'll never get this bread baked if you and Vivian don't hurry up!"

"We've chopped almost enough for you," Harry called to her. "Five more minutes, okay?"

"Well, okay," Aunt Caroline said. With that, she closed the back door, and Harry and Vivian went back to splitting the wood.

Harry and Vivian took turns swinging their axes into a chunk of wood to make a split in one end. Next they put the blade of an iron wedge in the split and tapped it several times with the blunt side of the ax. After that, they gave the wedge a solid blow with the blunt side of the ax, which caused the chunk to split in half. They repeated this with each smaller piece of wood until Harry thought they would go into the stove easily and not be too thick to burn. Then they brought the wood into the house.

Harry liked nothing better than to be in the kitchen when Aunt Caroline was baking, whether it was bread or pies or cakes. He thought Aunt Caroline had to be the best cook in the world, and she told Harry exactly what she was doing and why it was important.

"If you don't do it this way, Harry," she was always saying, "then it won't be fit to eat."

At that moment, the back door opened again, and Aunt Caroline stood there looking at them.

Quickly, Harry and Vivian gathered up as much stove wood as they could carry and ran for the back porch. Aunt Caroline held the door open, but she didn't say anything, and Harry could tell by the expression on her face that she was a little annoyed at them.

"Vivian, why don't you go pick up the sticks that we dropped?" Harry suggested. "I'll help Aunt Caroline put the wood in the stove."

Aunt Caroline took a deep breath and said, "Harry S. Truman, if you weren't such a gentleman, I'd be angry with you right now, because I'm off my baking schedule by several minutes."

"I'm sorry," Harry said. "This wood seems a little tougher than what Papa got last month."

"Well, I'll accept that excuse this time," Aunt Caroline said, "but next time you'll have to start splitting the wood sooner."

Harry winked at Mary Jane, who was in the corner of the kitchen, churning butter.

When Vivian got back with the sticks they had dropped, he was out of breath.

"I guess the two of you are all tuckered out from working so hard," Aunt Caroline said. "I think I have just the remedy for that."

"What?" Vivian asked.

"I just took a fresh batch of bread out of the oven," Aunt Caroline said. "How does a slice of that sound to you?"

"Delicious!" Harry said.

"May we have some of Mary Jane's butter on it?" Vivian asked.

Aunt Caroline looked over at Mary Jane and said, in a teasing voice, "Well, now, I think that if you ask your sister nicely, she might spread some of that wonderful yellow butter she just churned on the pieces of hot bread that I'm fixing to cut off for you."

Mary Jane slowly laid down the wooden paddle with which she had been stirring the butter. Without looking at either Harry or Vivian, she said, "I'm waiting."

"Waiting for what?" Vivian asked.

Mary Jane ignored Vivian's question. With a grin, she dipped out chunks of the butter and put them in a wooden bowl.

"Answer me, Mary Jane," Vivian said impatiently.

Harry, understanding that their sister was playing a little game with them, said, as sweetly as he could, "Mary Jane, would you *please* put some of your delicious butter on the slices of bread that Aunt Caroline is going to cut for us?"

At that, Mary Jane turned and gave them both a big smile. "Of course I will," she said. "You two have worked very hard this morning and you deserve to be the first to taste my wonderful butter."

Vivian looked at Harry and rolled his eyes. "Girls!" he muttered under his breath. "They make me tired."

Harry just smiled at him. Girls didn't make him tired. In fact, he had often thought about how much more he enjoyed listening to girls talk than boys. They were just more interesting.

Of course, when Harry was around girls his own age, he still found it difficult to overcome his shyness to enter into a conversation. The only girls he felt at ease with were his cousins Ethel and Nellie Noland. They were the daughters of Mr. Truman's sister Ella and her husband, Joseph Noland. Now that they lived in Independence, they were close enough for Harry to spend more time with them, and he thoroughly enjoyed doing so.

From time to time, Mrs. Truman would say that she thought the good Lord had really intended for Harry to be a girl, but Harry never took this as an insult, and his mother certainly never meant it to be. She was just making a comment based on what he liked to do and what he didn't like to do.

Harry knew that other boys who only wanted to talk to and listen to girls were sometimes called "sissies," but that had never happened to him. Sometimes boys teased him about his glasses, but they always had a certain respect for him and, to Harry, that was what really counted, not whether he was popular with the other guys.

Aunt Carolyn gave Vivian and Harry each a thick slice of warm bread, and Mary Jane spread them with the fresh butter. Harry sat down at the table to eat his, but Vivian asked, "Don't you want to go out to the barn, Harry? I think there are some new pigeons roosting up in the loft."

"Not now, Vivian, I want to talk to Aunt Caroline and Mary Jane," Harry said. "I may come out later."

"Okay," Vivian said.

Harry took a bite of his bread and butter. "Nobody bakes bread like you do, Aunt Caroline," he said. "This is better than cake."

"Thank you, Harry," Aunt Caroline said. She opened the oven door and put in two more loaves of bread dough. "The secret is having the oven just the right temperature, and you need somebody who can always be trusted to bring you a lot of good sticks of wood on time." She gave Harry a big grin, and Harry knew that she was teasing him.

When Harry finished eating his bread, he thought about going out to the barn to see if Vivian had located where the pigeons were roosting, but instead, he said, "Mary Jane, while you're churning that next batch of butter, I'll braid your hair, if you want."

"Oh, would you, Harry?" Mary Jane said. "Nobody can braid my hair like you, not even Mama."

Harry washed his hands, then pulled his chair over next to where Mary Jane was sitting.

Mary Jane gave Harry one of her big smiles. It melted his heart. Harry loved his sister, and he would do anything for her. Sometimes he had nightmares that something had happened to Mary Jane. He would wake up drenched in a cold sweat. When they were playing outside, Harry never took his eyes off her, for fear that she might hurt herself.

"I'm going to bake some pies now, Harry," Aunt Caroline said, "so while you're braiding Mary Jane's hair, I'll give you the secret of a good crust."

"Thank you, Aunt Caroline," Harry said. "If there's one thing I don't like, it's a tough crust."

Just then, Mrs. Truman came into the kitchen. "I noticed this morning that we were almost out of jams, jellies, and preserves, Caroline, so I'm going to make a list of the ones that I want Harry to bring in from the cellar."

"Okay, Miss Martha," Aunt Caroline said.

As Aunt Caroline revealed her pie crust

secret, Harry continued to braid Mary Jane's silky hair. Was there anything more wonderful, he wondered, than sitting in a cozy kitchen, listening to people talk?

Later, when the loaves of bread came out of the oven all golden brown, and the pies went into the oven to bake, Mrs. Truman handed Harry a piece of paper with the list of jams, jellies, and preserves to bring in from the cellar. "That cellar door is a bit contrary these days, so if you need any help, get Vivian, if you can find him."

"I can do it by myself, Mama," Harry assured her. "Vivian's up in the loft looking for pigeons."

Harry put his coat back on and headed out the back door to the cellar. Although not quite as big as the cellar on Grandma Young's farm, the Trumans' cellar was still large enough to store a lot of food that needed to be kept cool.

When Harry got to the cellar, he unlatched

the door, then pulled it up and locked it in place with the chain that was connected to it.

When the Trumans moved to the address on Waldo Avenue, one of the first things Mr. Truman did was put paving stones on the dirt steps to keep them from eroding. Harry and Vivian helped him. Together, they also shored up the ceiling with new timber, because the old wood had begun to rot, and built several new rows of shelves.

"I don't think the previous owner stored as much food down here as we'll be doing," Mr. Truman said when they were finished and he was surveying his work. "We have a lot of mouths to feed."

Harry didn't particularly like the musty smell that always greeted him when he went down into the cellar, but he was always amazed at how the temperature stayed constant. Sometimes, during the summer, when it was really hot outside, Vivian would play down in the cellar because he didn't mind getting dirty, but Harry would never join him. Harry knew that some people thought he was *too* neat, with his clothes and everything else, but so was his father. Mr. Truman liked everything to be perfect.

The jars of jams, jellies, and preserves were on the shelves at the back of the cellar, right where Harry had put them the previous summer. He could still smell the aroma of the cooking fruit, as Aunt Caroline and his mother worked from early in the morning until late at night, getting all of the ripened fruit into the jars. Sometimes, Uncle Harry would bring Grandma Young to help them, and it was during those times when Harry relived life on the farm.

Harry glanced down at his list, noted again what his mother wanted, and then begin taking the jars off the shelves. He probably should have asked Vivian to help, he decided, because he soon had both hands full.

If I'm careful, Harry decided, *I can make it.*

He checked his mother's list one last time, then he started back up the cellar steps.

When Harry was aboveground again, he balanced one foot on the rim of the door frame and shifted most of the jars to his left hand so he could unhook the door with his right to shut it. But the chain slipped out of his hand, and the door fell in place.

Harry's brain told him that something awful had happened, but it took a few seconds for it to register fully, and then all of a sudden he felt an excruciating pain in the big toe of his left foot. The cellar door had slammed on his foot.

Harry dropped the jars.

He managed to lift the door just enough to pull out his foot, then he fell to the ground.

"Mama! Papa!" he cried. "Help me, please!"

Vivian, who was returning from the barn, ran up to him. "What's wrong, Harry?" he asked anxiously.

Inside his shoe, Harry could feel a warmth

spreading around his toes, and he knew that wasn't good. "It's my big toe," Harry gasped. "The cellar door slammed shut on it, and I think it may be cut badly."

"I'll get Mama and Papa," Vivian said. He raced for the back porch and into the house.

Within seconds, the entire family had gathered around Harry. Mr. Truman removed Harry's boot. His sock was soaked in blood.

"Oh, Harry!" Mrs. Truman cried. She helped Mr. Truman carefully remove the sock. The end of Harry's big toe had been severed. "Caroline, you and Mary Jane get some blankets so we can cover Harry up and keep him warm," Mrs. Truman said. "John, you get Dr. Twyman, and I'll hold the end of the toe in place until he gets here, and maybe we can save it."

Harry began to feel light-headed at the sight of the blood and at thinking about what had just happened, so when Aunt Caroline returned with the blankets and his mother had made him as comfortable as she could, he let himself fall into a state somewhere between waking and sleeping.

When he came to he was in his bed, but his foot was throbbing unmercifully. His mother was sitting in a chair beside him.

Mrs. Truman squeezed Harry's hand. "The doctor thinks he was able to save the end of your toe," she said. "He told us that he put a coating of something that's called crystalline iodoform on it, and then he bandaged it carefully."

"It was my fault, Mama," Harry said, almost in tears. "I should have asked Vivian to help me, but I thought I could carry everything myself."

"This was just a bad accident, Harry, and there is no one to blame for anything," Mrs. Truman said, smoothing his hair back out of his eyes.

Harry had to stay in bed for a couple of weeks. After that he was able to hobble to the kitchen table for a meal, or just to listen to Aunt Caroline talk about what she was cooking that day. Harry also noticed that the shelf where the jams, jellies, and preserves were kept had been restocked, but he didn't ask who had done it. He didn't want to think about all of the jars he had broken, wasting the good food inside, or about the day when the door had slammed on his foot.

Within a month, Harry's toe was well enough that he could wear a loose-fitting slipper on the injured foot, so one day, at Vivian's request and with his mother's blessing, Harry went out to the barn to see the pigeons that had captured Vivian's imagination and most of his time for the past few weeks.

It was slow going, but with Vivian's help, Harry managed to climb the ladder to the hayloft. Harry wasn't as interested in seeing the pigeons as he was in seeing Vivian's reaction to them. Harry was well aware that he had changed a lot since his family had left the farm. Back then, everything connected with farm life, including being around all kinds of animals, was what had interested him the most, but now, since they had been living in Independence, Harry had gotten a taste of what it meant to be educated, and he found himself wanting to spend more time with books than with animals.

Harry stayed with Vivian in the hayloft for a couple of hours, listening to him talk about the pigeons, which he had even given names.

When Vivian asked him if he was ready to go back to the house, Harry told him yes. He made sure that he thanked his brother for sharing his new animals with him, but Harry could hardly wait to start a new book about Thomas Jefferson, the third president of the United States.

Harry Tries to Understand His Father

Sometimes Harry had a difficult time under-standing why he didn't feel as close to his father as he did to his mother. So one spring day in 1894, he made a conscious decision to try harder to bond with his father.

It was no secret to anybody, family or friends, that Harry adored his mother. He was always eager to please her and he never wanted to see her unhappy about anything. For that reason, Harry was referred to as "his mama's boy." With family, there was nothing unkind about that label. Even with friends, it was mostly an expression of how people viewed Harry's relationship with Mrs. Truman.

But Harry knew that he had more in common with his father than most of the Trumans' friends realized, since family members, if they were pressed, would often say of Harry's behavior, "He's a real Truman, that boy, because that's exactly what John did at his age."

Part of Harry's plan included offering to help his father with whatever work he was doing that particular day, even if it meant hard labor or, worse, being bored.

The first day Harry put his plan into effect was almost the last day, too, because when John Truman was trading horses with a neighbor, Harry let a harness slip, which caused a deep gash on the horse's neck. That ended the deal right then, and John Truman was furious.

"If you can't do it right, Harry, then I don't need you around to mess it up for me," his

father admonished him. "Now, that horse is good to no one."

"It was an accident, Papa," Harry tried to explain. "I just pulled too hard. I won't do that again."

"There won't be a next time, Harry," his father said. "I can't afford to have you ruin another horse trade for me."

Harry felt cut to the quick by his father's stinging remarks, but he stuck it out, doctoring the horse himself without his father's knowledge. It wasn't long until the gash had healed. When Harry showed it to his father, he received what almost amounted to an apology.

Harry also believed he got his attitude about women from his father. Like many men of that time, John Truman would not tolerate another man's making any kind of negative comment toward a woman. Anyone who did so immediately got into trouble.

John Truman wasn't above harming a man

physically. Once, in the Jackson County courthouse, a lawyer called John Truman a liar, and Harry watched as his father slugged the man and chased him out of the building and into the street. Harry knew that he had a temper almost as bad as his father's, but for some reason, probably from being around his mother's calming influence, he was able to keep it in check.

Although it seemed to bother Vivian that Mary Jane was their father's favorite, it made sense to Harry due to John Truman's attitude toward women. Harry told Vivian that it really shouldn't bother him, either.

"That's easy for you to say, Harry," Vivian admonished him. "You're mother's favorite!" With tears in his eyes, Vivian added, "Mary Jane is even your favorite. I'm nobody's favorite."

"That's not true, Vivian," Harry said. "It's just not true."

How could Harry tell Vivian that although

he adored Mary Jane, if he admitted it to himself, he had just recently decided that part of the reason he spent so much time with Mary Jane was because he knew it would meet with their father's approval? He was sure of his mother's love, 100 percent, but deep down, he wasn't sure of his father's love, and he wanted that more than almost anything else.

Harry admired his father's business sense. John Truman was involved in a lot of ventures, and it seemed to Harry that almost everything his father touched turned to money.

John Truman farmed some rented land just south of Independence, and hired a black man, Letch Simpson, to help him. Sometimes Harry went with them.

"I thought when we left the farm you'd give up farming, John," Mrs. Truman said one day. "It seems to me that you're spending more time at that now than you did when we lived with my parents."

"That's not true, Mattie," Mr. Truman countered.

Harry often heard this argument from his mother. Although most of the time Mrs. Truman just accepted the fact that sometimes she had to act as both father and mother, there were other times when her resentment spilled out.

If John Truman wasn't farming, he was dealing in real estate, a growing business in the booming Kansas City area. Often, he'd hitch up the horse and buggy and he and Harry would drive all around the area, with Mr. Truman telling Harry why he thought certain property was good and why he thought other property was bad. Harry learned a lot during these trips and, later, when school was back in session, he would take different routes every morning and every evening, appraising the houses and businesses he passed.

To Harry, his family was very well off. He realized that they didn't have as much money as some of the other people around—most notably Bess Wallace's family—but they were able to hire more servants to take care of the household, acquire as many books as they wanted, and have studio photographs taken quite often.

John Truman soon added inventor to his list of skills, and Harry tried to help him in his workshop. Unfortunately, this was a very frustrating time, because Harry had begun to tire of trying to keep up with his father in order to gain his approval.

One day, when Harry's father announced that he was going to talk to some people at the Chicago & Alton Railroad about one of his inventions, an automated railroad switch, he invited Harry to accompany him, knowing of Harry's love of trains. But Harry said he was busy, that he had some reading to catch up on. His father went by himself.

Later, when Harry learned from his mother that the railroad had turned his father down because he had asked for too much money, Harry blamed himself, thinking that his refusal to go might have upset his father more than he realized.

John Truman never spoke of the matter to Harry, and it was a long time before he ever asked him to go on any more business ventures.

Piano Lessons

One Friday morning in 1896, when Harry was twelve years old, Mrs. Truman announced that they were going to Kansas City to buy a piano.

Harry had overheard his mother talking to his father the night before, telling him that they had the money for a piano and that with all the people they had hired to help take care of their house and property, thanks to their prosperity from John Truman's various business ventures, she now had the time to resume playing the piano.

"The children don't need me every minute of the day anymore, John," Mrs. Truman said. "I have missed playing the piano, so I think it's time we buy one for the parlor."

Harry knew that having a piano in the parlor was considered part of the "good life" in America, meaning it was a symbol that your family was prosperous. It was also considered very wholesome home entertainment. When Harry had visited the homes of other members of the Waldo Avenue Gang, he had noticed that the piano was at the center of life in the parlor. From time to time, the mothers of his friends or the girls themselves had entertained the gang with some of the popular songs of the time.

The next day, the Truman family rode into Kansas City to the Miller Music Company, a large store just east of the downtown area, where several other families in Independence had purchased their pianos.

"I want an upright Kimball, just like the one

the Lowes have. I visited them a couple of weeks ago, and Mrs. Lowe and Cellie played me several pieces on theirs," Mrs. Truman said. "I think it has a wonderfully clear tone to it."

"I don't really know anything about pianos, Mama, but I know I enjoy hearing Cellie when she plays," Harry said, "and I think that Ara's family has a Kimball too."

"Well, I think we should look at all of the pianos before we make a decision on which one to get," Mr. Truman said. "We shouldn't buy a piano just because other people have one like it."

Harry noticed his mother purse her lips. "Well, we'll see, John," she said.

"I like fast music, but I don't want to hear any of that classical stuff," Vivian said. "I hope I don't have to start listening to that all the time."

"Oh, Vivian, you need to learn to like all kinds of music," Mary Jane said. "It's the only way to grow as a person."

Vivian gave Mary Jane an exasperated look and leaned forward to Mrs. Truman. "Mama, if you let Mary Jane play that classical music all the time, I'm going to move out to the barn."

"I don't even know how to play the piano yet, Vivian," Mary Jane said.

Harry tapped Vivian on the shoulder. "We'll give you plenty of warning, so you'll know when it's time to go to the barn," he said. He gave Vivian a big grin. "Don't worry, Vivian, Mama likes all kinds of music, and I'm sure she'll play some of the things that you enjoy."

"Yes, I will, Vivian," Mrs. Truman assured him.

When the Trumans arrived at the Miller Music Company, Harry was amazed at how many different types of musical instruments the store sold. He had never even heard of most of them before. It was hard to believe that somewhere in the Kansas City area there were people making music from instruments just like these.

After looking at every piano available, the Trumans finally decided on the one they wanted. It was an upright Kimball, and it cost John Truman two hundred dollars!

When the piano was delivered three days later, it was a cause for celebration. Several neighbors were on hand to witness its arrival. After the movers had set it in the middle of the parlor, with very specific directions from Mrs. Truman, there was a spontaneous concert. As she had promised, Mrs. Truman played some fast music for Vivian, but when she started a piece by Chopin, Harry noticed that Vivian slipped quietly out of the parlor. Harry was pretty sure Vivian did that more for show than for anything else, just to prove that he'd meant what he'd said.

Over the next few weeks, Harry seemed drawn to the piano. Several times a day, he requested that his mother stop what she was doing and play something on the piano.

"Harry, I'll never get any work done if I keep doing this," she told him one afternoon. Suddenly a big smile appeared on her face. "Why don't I teach you how to play the piano, so you can hear whatever you want to hear?"

Harry was flabbergasted. That idea had never occurred to him. He didn't know any other boys who played the piano. It was always their mothers and their sisters.

"Would you really?" he managed to say.

Mrs. Truman nodded. "I had planned to teach Mary Jane, but she doesn't seem to have any interest in learning," she said, "and there's no sense in wasting her time—or mine—if it's not something she wants to do."

"Oh, Mama!" Harry exclaimed. "I really do want to learn how to play the piano."

"Well, if you'll let me finish what I was doing, then we'll start your lessons tonight, after dinner," Mrs. Truman said. "How about that?"

"I'm not sure I can wait that long," Harry said with a grin, "but I'll try."

Mrs. Truman laughed. "I have an idea. Why don't you just sit down now and do some scales?" she said. "Just lightly go up and down the keys with your fingers, listening to the sound each one makes. It's important that you train your ear to recognize each note."

For most of the rest of the day, Harry sat at the piano, listening carefully to the sound of each key. Over and over, he went up and down the keyboard. From time to time, he'd close his eyes and randomly select a key to strike. With his eyes still closed, he'd try to decide which note it was. It wasn't long before he was getting every one of them right.

True to her word, after dinner that night, Mrs. Truman gave Harry his first piano lesson. It wasn't long, though, before she felt that she had taught Harry everything she knew.

"I talked to Miss Burrus next door today,

Harry. I told her that you have a talent for music," his mother said. "All of her other pupils are young ladies, but she said that if you want to learn, she would be willing to give you regular lessons because you are such a nice young man."

From that point on, Harry's life took a different turn. He rearranged his daily routine in order to accommodate piano practice.

On the first morning after his first lesson with Miss Burrus, Mrs. Truman opened the door to his room and whispered, "Harry, it's five o'clock. You told me to get you up so you could practice the piano. Do you remember that?"

Harry slowly sat up in bed and rubbed his eyes. "Yes, Mama, I remember." He climbed out of bed, washed his face in the basin on top of his chest, dressed quietly so as not to disturb Vivian, and went downstairs to the parlor to practice.

Miss Burrus had told Harry that it was very

important that he practice the scales and do finger exercises before he worked on any piece of music, so that's what he did, even though by now he found scales boring. He respected Miss Burrus's musical knowledge, so he planned to follow her directions to the letter.

Harry checked the grandfather clock standing against the far wall. It was almost time for breakfast. He needed to switch to the musical selections Miss Burrus had included in this lesson. First, there was a simple piece from Mozart, which he breezed through easily. That was followed by something more difficult from Bach. He finished just as Vivian came downstairs.

"Were you playing some of that classical stuff, Harry?" Vivian asked.

Harry quickly played a scale that sounded as if it could be from the kind of music Vivian liked. "You mean this?" he asked.

Vivian gave him a funny look. "I guess I

was dreaming, then, because that's not what I heard."

"I guess you were," Harry told him.

When Harry and Vivian went into the kitchen, the rest of the family were seated around the table. Aunt Caroline had just started to serve them.

"You're learning to play really well, Harry," Mr. Truman said. "We were enjoying listening to you play those classical pieces."

"Thanks, Papa," Harry said.

Vivian gave Harry a dirty look but didn't say anything, because at that moment, Aunt Caroline set a huge stack of pancakes in front of him.

After Harry and Vivian had finished breakfast, they headed out to the barn to milk the three cows that John Truman kept to make sure the family had fresh milk, cream, and butter.

When they finished milking and had stored the milk away in a room where their father kept chunks of ice, Harry and Vivian herded the three cows out of the barn to a gate that led to a side street so they could take them to a pasture about three miles from their house.

"Look at them, Harry," Vivian said as the cows started down the road without having to be coaxed. "They know where they're going."

Harry nodded. "They're hungry, and it's a good pasture, with lots of tall grass," he said. "I wouldn't have to herd you, either, Vivian, if you were headed to an ice-cream parlor."

"That's right," Vivian agreed.

A mile down the road, they passed one of their father's friends, William Lancaster, who called, "There go two future Missouri farmers!"

Vivian and Harry waved back.

"I think that's probably what I want to be, Harry," Vivian said. "I like all the friends we have in town, but sometimes I miss living on a real farm."

"Do you?" Harry said. "You never told me that."

"It's just something I've been thinking about lately," Vivian said. "I just like the smell of the barn." He turned to Harry. "It reminds me of Grandpa and Grandma Young's farm. Does that sound silly?"

"I don't think it sounds silly at all, Vivian," Harry said. "I know exactly what you mean."

"What if we both went back together, Harry?" Vivian said excitedly. "It would be just like it used to be."

"Well, you never can tell what life holds for you, Vivian," Harry said. "Who knows? That might just happen one of these days."

Harry's reply seemed to satisfy Vivian, but Harry himself wasn't happy with his answer. He wasn't deceiving Vivian, he knew, because he still found himself remembering farm life fondly, and he knew that the land would always be in his blood. But he wasn't sure he could ever return there to live and work full-time. His life had changed too much since the family had moved to Independence. There were too many things in his life now that he could never give up: School. Books. Music.

When Harry and Vivian got back to their house, they went straight to the barn to finish their chores.

Harry took care of his Shetland pony, and Vivian started feeding their father's horses. When Harry finished with his pony, he helped Vivian pump water to fill the watering trough.

While the horses were eating, Harry and Vivian started to curry them. Harry enjoyed making their coats look smooth and shiny.

When they were finished they started toward the house, but noticed their father repairing a nearby fence.

"Do you need any help, Papa?" Harry called.

"I'm just about finished with this," Mr. Truman said, "but the weeds have almost overtaken your mother's garden, so I would like for you to hoe that for me."

"We'll do that, Papa!" Vivian shouted.

Hoeing and weeding was what Harry called mindless work. He could do it without thinking, leaving his mind free to wander and think about other things. As he went up and down the rows, carefully chopping the weeds from the carrots, the onions, the squash, and the corn, he thought about how wonderful these last few years had been. Sometimes it scared him that each year brought more happiness. In another year, he'd be starting high school. Would he feel the same about his life after he was out of school? he wondered.

High School

Harry started high school in the autumn of 1897. He had dreamed of this day almost since his family had first moved to Independence.

Once, when he and his father were on their way to a blacksmith's to buy some horseshoes, they drove past Independence High School during the noon break. Students were milling around outside, sitting on the grass or standing under trees talking.

"You'll be doing that one of these days," Mr. Truman told Harry. With a sigh, he added, "It's hard to believe that you'll be as big as some of those boys out there."

Harry found it hard to believe, too, when he saw how big the boys were, but he certainly liked that idea. At the moment, though, that time seemed so far away that it was almost unreal.

Now, after having spent most of the day at Independence High School registering for his classes, Harry was at the Noland house, visiting with his cousins Ethel and Nellie. He wanted to ask them questions about the teachers he would have that first year.

"I have Mr. Hankins for English," Harry told them. "What can you tell me about him?"

"You're lucky, Harry. He's a very good teacher. I wish I had had Mr. Hankins for freshman English," Ethel said. "Unfortunately, I had Miss Johnson, and I almost fell asleep in every class."

"I had Mr. Hankins," Nellie said. "You'll learn a lot in his class."

Harry looked down at his schedule. "Miss

Bonner for math," he said. "Anything I should know?"

"Oh, Harry, why are we doing this?" Nellie teased. "You'll do well in anybody's class."

Harry thought that was probably true, because he loved school and he always studied hard, but just as with almost any person, it didn't hurt to know a teacher's peculiarities.

"I don't know Miss Bonner," Ethel said. "I think she's new this year."

"There must be a lot of new teachers at the school," Harry said. "I heard some of the other kids talking about it."

"Well, Independence is growing, Harry," Nellie said, "so that means more students, and more students mean more teachers."

"I think you'd make a good teacher, Nellie," Harry said. "I could listen to you talk for a whole hour."

"Oh, Harry, what a nice thing to say," Nellie said. She patted him on the arm. "You're a dear."

Harry stayed until it was almost dinner-time. Naturally, he was invited to eat with the Nolands, but he declined the invitation, saying he'd better head home before his parents wondered what had happened to him.

He left the Nolands' house on Maple Street and walked the short distance to his house. He always hated leaving Ethel and Nellie. When he was there, he felt as much at home as he did in his own house. Sometimes he thought it would be wonderful to live with the Nolands. Ethel and Nellie were really the only close friends he had. They were good-natured, read all of the time just like he did, and were interested in and could talk about almost everything. It also wasn't hard for Harry to tell that they felt the same way about him. Beyond that, though, Ethel had always seemed to understand him more than anyone else did—even his mother. They had a special unspoken connection.

The next morning, Harry was dressed an hour earlier than usual. He was in the kitchen fixing his own breakfast when Aunt Caroline came in.

"What's wrong with you?" she asked, giving him a concerned look. "You look jittery."

"Butterflies, I guess, Aunt Caroline," Harry admitted. "I don't know why."

"Well, that's the way it is sometimes when you start something new, and I hear tell that high school is a lot different from grade school," Aunt Caroline said, "although it's not from experience, because I never went to any kind of school. I learned what I know at my mama's knee, God rest her soul."

"Aunt Caroline, did you ever wish that you could have gone to school?" Harry asked.

Aunt Caroline nodded. "When I was just a little girl, there was a white doctor who came to my house to see my ailing grandfather," she said, "and I never forgot how kind, how gentle he was to that old man, and I remembered thinking that when I grew up, I wanted to be a doctor too." She shrugged her shoulders. "Of course, it didn't happen, and what happened happened, and that's all there is to it."

Harry hugged her. "When I grow up, I'm going to make sure that all people have the chance to be what they want to be," he said.

Just then, Mrs. Truman came into the kitchen. "Well, Harry, how long have you been up?" she asked.

"He's been up long enough to help me cook breakfast," Aunt Caroline said. "We've been talking about how much energy it takes to go to high school."

Harry looked up at the clock. "I'm going to leave now," he said. "I thought maybe I'd meet up with some of the Waldo Avenue Gang going early too."

Just as Harry was leaving, the rest of the family came into the kitchen and wished him good luck on his first day of high school.

Harry thanked them and started down the sidewalk.

The streets were empty, though, and he realized that the rest of the Waldo Avenue Gang had decided that there wasn't any need to get to school earlier than necessary.

Harry didn't know for sure who would be in his classes this year, but he hoped there would be at least somebody he knew. Would the Waldo Avenue Gang even stay together this year? he wondered. Or would they all form other friendships that would separate them from one another?

Paul Bryant lived on the other side of Waldo Avenue, on the campus of little Woodland College for Women, because his father was the college's president. But Paul had spent part of the summer in Minnesota, so he hadn't been around to do a lot of the things the gang often did when school was out.

Fielding Houchens was the son of the Baptist minister, and since their house and the Trumans' house backed onto the same alley, Harry and Fielding would sometimes talk about what was happening in Independence, but that was about all they had done.

Harry had seen Elmer Twyman several times this summer, when Elmer and Dr. Twyman passed Harry on their way to visit patients. They would wave at one another. Elmer had told Harry that he wanted to be a doctor, so this summer he was spending more time watching what his father did.

Tasker Taylor had dropped by several times during the summer to show Harry some of his new sketches. Harry thought Tasker could draw better than anyone he knew. Tasker wanted to go to art school in New York City when he finished high school, but his parents were against it. Tasker told Harry they didn't think he could make a living at it. "You should follow your dream," Harry told him.

When it came right down to it, the only

member of the gang Harry had made an effort to see during the summer was Charlie Ross. Harry had always secretly wished he were as tall as Charlie. With most people, Charlie was incredibly shy, but around Harry, he knew he was with a kindred spirit. Like Harry, Charlie read everything he could get his hands on. They were always recommending new books to each other.

Would things change even more, Harry wondered, as soon as his first class started?

Harry needn't have worried. His English class with Mr. Hankins was first period, and Tasker, Charlie, and Paul were in it. So was Bess. Once the class started, Harry knew that not only were Nellie and Ethel right about Mr. Hawkins, but that the friendships he had made when his family first arrived in Independence wouldn't change in any way. From the friendly banter in class, Harry decided that everyone knew that their friendships would only deepen.

At noon, after they had eaten, Paul, Fielding, Elmer, Tasker, Charlie, and Harry decided to stroll around the grounds of the high school, just to familiarize themselves with the place where they'd be spending the next four years.

After one complete circle, they decided to rest since the day was warm.

They sat on the grass under the maple with the biggest shade and started giving their impressions of what had happened during the morning classes.

Harry looked up just as a buggy was passing by carrying a man and a boy. Harry suddenly remembered that day long ago, when that had been he and his father.

Was the father telling his son the same thing Mr. Truman had told Harry, that in just a few years he'd be one of those boys sitting out there under that tree?

Harry smiled to himself.

Just then, a bell rang.

Harry stood up. "Well," he said to the rest of his friends, "we'd better hurry or we'll be late for math."

After school, Harry waited outside for his cousin Ethel, who was a year ahead of him and was late as usual, so he could walk home with her.

"Tell me everything that happened today," Ethel said.

"Well, you were right about Mr. Hawkins. He's a great teacher," Harry told her. "I'm really excited about all the books we're going to read in his class."

"Oh, Harry, isn't high school fun?" Ethel said, grabbing his arm and squeezing it. "I just feel so much more . . . *intellectual*." She laughed. "Don't you?"

Harry grinned. "I guess," he said.

"Don't be so modest," Ethel said. "I think you should . . ." She stopped talking and looked at him. "We've come to Delaware

Street, Harry. You know who lives on Delaware Street, don't you?"

Harry blushed. "Of course, I do, Ethel," he said. "Bess does."

"Let's take a little detour, Harry," Ethel suggested. "We might just see Bess on the front porch having a glass of lemonade."

"Oh, no, let's not do that," Harry protested. "She'll think I'm spying on her."

"Well, you are, Harry Truman," Ethel said.

"Don't tease me, Ethel," Harry said. "When it comes to Bess, I don't like it."

"I'm not teasing you, Harry. I'm just trying to get you to realize that Bess Wallace is one of the most popular girls in Independence," Ethel told him frankly. She grabbed his hand. "If you don't let her know that you like her, someone else will."

They were now walking up North Delaware Street in the direction of Bess's house.

"I think she knows I like her," Harry said. "I talk to her occasionally."

"Is she still sitting behind you in class?" Ethel asked.

Harry smiled and nodded. "I have four classes with her, and she sits behind me in each one," he said.

Harry had never been able to believe his good fortune. Ever since he had switched to the Columbian School in the fourth grade, Bess had sat immediately behind him in class, because of the alphabetical seating arrangement.

But the closer Harry and Ethel got to Bess's house, the more nervous Harry became.

"She'll know what I'm doing, Ethel," Harry complained. "I don't think this is a good idea."

Ethel tightened her grip on Harry's arm. "I'm a girl, Harry, and I do think this is a good idea," she told him firmly.

Bess's house was only two and a half blocks from Harry's, but it might as well have been in another world. The houses in Bess's neighborhood were all very large and had sidewalks

178

of hexagonal flagstone. The people who lived along North Delaware Street were the upper crust of Independence, Harry knew. At Christmas, they gave their friends gifts wrapped in beautiful paper. The boys wore tuxedos, and the girls wore silk dresses to formal parties and dances—the ones that Harry was never invited to. Harry—consciously or subconsciously, he wasn't sure—never walked past Bess's house by himself. He always felt just too conspicuous.

Now, as they passed in front of the tall frame house with the bur oak shading the lawn, Harry could hardly breathe. Out of the corner of his right eye he could tell that no one was sitting on the porch, but he was just positive that Bess was at a window on one of the upper floors, watching them now, and wondering why in the world Harry S. Truman was walking past his house with his cousin Ethel.

Harry tried to pick up the pace, but Ethel wouldn't let him.

"I have a suggestion, Harry," Ethel said without looking at him. "Why don't you make a point of being in front of the school one day next week, as Bess starts home, and ask her if you could carry her books for her?"

Finally, they had passed Bess's house, and Harry started breathing more easily.

"What if she says no, Ethel?" Harry asked.

"Well, Harry, I guess you'll just never know until you ask her, will you?" Ethel said.

For several minutes, Harry said nothing. Then, just as they turned a corner onto a street that would take them to the Noland house, Harry said, "Ethel, I think in the next few weeks I just might."

America's Heartland

By the time Harry got home, he had made a decision. He was going to learn as much about Independence as he could. He was going to know everything there was to know about everybody.

He and his family had been in Independence for several years now, but Harry didn't really know all that much about the town. He still felt as though he were on the outside looking in, and he didn't want to feel that way. If he was going to live in Independence for the rest of his life—and at the moment, he didn't see any reason why that would change—then he wanted to be a real part of everyday life there.

Harry decided that the best place to start would be the Independence Public Library, a two-room house next door to the high school.

He had become friends with the librarian, Miss Carrie Wallace, a charming and cultured lady, who used to teach English at Independence High School. Miss Wallace was also Bess's cousin, which Harry admitted to himself might be one of the reasons he spent so much time at the library.

Saturday morning, he was at the front door of the library just as Miss Wallace arrived.

"Oh, my goodness, Harry," Miss Wallace exclaimed when she saw him, "there must be something really special that you need, for you to be here so early. Do you have a term paper due Monday?"

"No, ma'am," Harry told her. "I wanted to talk to you about Independence."

182

"Well, if there's one thing I can talk about for hours, it's Independence, because I've lived here all of my life," Miss Wallace said. She unlocked the front door, and she and Harry went inside. "Let me finish my morning responsibilities and then we'll talk." Miss Wallace gave Harry a big smile. "Most of my patrons won't be in this early."

Harry loved the way libraries smelled. There was something very comforting about it. While he waited for Miss Wallace to finish her tasks, he browsed the section of recently acquired books. He saw several historical titles that he knew he wanted to read.

Finally, Miss Wallace was ready. "I thought we'd sit over here, in the 'parlor,'" she said as she led Harry to a far corner of the library. "It's much more comfortable, and I'll still be able to see any patrons who might arrive earlier than expected."

Harry had seen the "parlor" before, but had never sat in any of the chairs there. Frankly, he thought, it looked too intimidating. It had an Oriental rug on the floor. Against the wall was a bookcase with glass doors. There was a coffee table in front of a sofa that had an ornately carved wooden back. There were two side chairs, with the same patterns. Once, Harry had seen two elderly ladies there, looking through several books that Miss Wallace had brought to them. Harry hadn't recognized the ladies, but from their appearance he was sure they were some of the wealthier residents of Independence. Now, with what he wanted to discuss with Miss Wallace, the parlor seemed like the most appropriate place.

Miss Wallace and Harry sat in side chairs, across from each other, with the coffee table between them, and Miss Wallace served tea from a silver service on the coffee table.

Miss Wallace sipped her tea. "Well, now, Harry, why do you want to know so much about Independence?"

Harry set his teacup in the saucer and

replied, "I don't want to feel like an outsider. I want to be able to walk down any street and feel as though I belong there."

Miss Wallace smiled. "Would one of those streets be North Delaware?" she asked.

Harry saw the twinkle in her eyes, but he still felt himself blushing.

"Your cousins Ethel and Nellie come to the library a lot. We've been friends for a long time," Miss Wallace said. "They've never betrayed any secrets, Harry, but we girls do talk about such things."

Harry grinned. "Well, I think that I've just learned something about Independence," he said. "It's the kind of town where everybody knows everybody and everybody's business."

Miss Wallace nodded. "And to some people that may sound bad, and Independence certainly does have its share of nosy people," she said, "but to me that means we all care about one another, and Ethel and Nellie certainly care about you."

"I know," Harry said. "I care very much about them, too."

Miss Wallace set her cup down. "Independence is changing, Harry, but thank goodness not as much as Kansas City," she said. "We're still a churchgoing, conservative people who are rooted to our past."

"There's nothing wrong with that," Harry said. "The people in Kansas City don't seem to know or care who their neighbors are."

"Well, I'm not sure it's that they don't care," Miss Wallace said, "but they're just too busy making money to get to know them."

Harry nodded.

"I've traveled in the South some, Harry. Alabama, Mississippi, Georgia," Miss Wallace said, "and I think if you moved Independence lock, stock, and barrel to one of those states, it would take several years for people to realize what had happened. It's much more Southern than Midwestern." She paused and looked at Harry. "If I start to bore you with my reminiscing, you will stop me, won't you? I sometimes get carried away when it comes to talking about Independence."

"What you're telling me is what I want to know, Miss Wallace," Harry assured her.

For the rest of the morning, with only an occasional interruption from library patrons, Miss Wallace regaled Harry with the history of Independence.

At the end of the Civil War, in 1865, Independence began to grow. The coming of the railroad was a major reason why. Another reason was nearby Kansas City. There were a lot of people who didn't mind working there, because there was a lot of money to be made, but at the end of the day those same people wanted to live somewhere else, and Independence proved inviting.

But all of the business growth wasn't just in Kansas City. There were several local businessmen whose enterprises also had a direct effect on the personality of Independence.

The Bullenes, the Sawyers, the Gates, the Waggoners, the Swopes, and the Vailes all built large houses for their families that became showplaces and centers of Independence society.

The Bullenes were part of the family that had founded the most popular dry goods store in Kansas City: Emery, Bird, Thayer. The Bullenes were a very good example of people who made their money in Kansas City but who preferred to live in Independence.

Aaron Sawyer headed the Bank of Independence. Since in business matters the bank was more conservative than some of the banks in Kansas City, it attracted a lot of customers who decided their money would be safer there.

George Porterfield Gates, who was Bess Wallace's grandfather, was a partner in the Waggoner-Gates Milling Company, founded in 1866. The company made Queen of the Pantry Flour, which was known throughout the Midwest as the best flour in the country.

Mr. Gates had come to Independence by way of Vermont and Illinois, so initially there were some people in town who considered him a Yankee. But he had all of the charm and acumen of a Southern gentlemen, so that label was soon forgotten. Two years after he joined Mr. Waggoner in the milling business in 1883, he began remodeling his house at the corner of North Delaware Street and Blue Avenue. When he finished, what had been a relatively modest house now had fourteen rooms, verandas in front and in back, tinted glass in the front bay windows, a slate roof, gas lighting, and hot and cold running water. People would drive their buggies and carriages from many miles away just to gaze at this magnificent house.

William Waggoner, Gates's partner, had an even grander house, which was located across from the mill on Pacific Street. It was on a knoll in a parklike setting of over twenty acres.

The Swopes lived in a house on South Pleasant Street that had a ballroom on the top floor.

But it was the Vaile house on North Liberty that was the talk of the town. It was a towering, stone-trimmed, redbrick Victorian mansion with thirty-one rooms.

Independence at the end of the nineteenth century was a very pleasant place to live. The main streets were paved, clean, and shaded by magnificent large trees of every variety that grew in western Missouri. On summer evenings, the residents would sit on their front porches to enjoy a respite from the heat of the day, and talk about upcoming parties; local, state, and national politics; or, in general, just how wonderful it was to live in Independence. Some of the wealthier residents would also talk about their recent travels in Europe or what they had seen in other states.

When winter came, there was a soft glow

of gas and oil lamps from inside the houses in the town, adding to its gentle impression. Residents much preferred this to the harshness of all the electric lights in Kansas City, even though there was a new electric plant under construction in Independence.

In Independence, there were certain precepts that everyone lived by:

Honesty is the best policy.

Make yourself useful to everyone.

If something is going to be worthwhile, it'll require a lot of effort.

If at first you don't succeed, try, try again.

Never, ever give up.

"Thank you so much, Miss Wallace, for helping me understand Independence," Harry said. "It's a wonderful town, and I'm proud to be from here."

"You're welcome, Harry, and please come again," Miss Wallace said. "We'll have tea and talk about anything else you'd like to discuss."

"That would be a distinct pleasure, Miss Wallace," Harry assured her.

As Harry left the library, he thought of some of the other sayings that he had heard all of his life that he considered articles of faith to live by:

Children are a reflection of their parents.

Honor thy father and mother.

A good name is rather to be chosen than great riches.

Be of good cheer.

Say what you mean, mean what you say.

Keep your word.

Never get too big for your britches.

Never forget a friend.

As Harry's house on Waldo Avenue came into view, he made a vow. "I can't force everyone else to live by these rules, but I can certainly force myself, and that is exactly what I plan to do!"

Harry Gets His First Real Job

Harry knew that the heart of Independence was the town square, and at the center of the square was the Jackson County courthouse, a tall Victorian building, with a mansard-roofed clock tower five stories tall. It was home to most of the county's government officials, who were solidly Democratic.

Around the square were stores selling almost anything a resident of Independence could possibly need. Harry had often heard people say that if you couldn't find it on the square, then you probably didn't need it, but if you just had to have it, then you could take the train to Kansas City.

There were four drugstores, two saloons, A. J. Bundschu's Department Store, two barbershops, a theater, an opera house, a shoe store, a bakery, an ice-cream parlor, a jewelry store, a bookshop, two grocery stores, the Hotel Metropolitan, H. W. Rummel's harness and saddle shop, and a dry goods store. There were also three banks, standing prominently on three different corners. Upstairs, above the banks, were various law and dental offices and Miss Dunlap's dancing classes. Just off the square was a lumberyard, the Western Union offices, a barbershop for blacks, two livery stables, a feed store, the town jail, and the railroad station.

In September 1898, when Harry was fourteen, he decided he wanted a job at one of the businesses on the square, so he could be at the heart of what was happening in Independence.

It was quite common for people to stroll

around the square in the evenings, during the spring, summer, and early fall, so one evening, Harry asked Ethel and Nellie to walk with him to town while he decided where he wanted to work.

"I don't really think that's the way it's done, Harry," Nellie said. "I think you have to apply for a job and then the owner of the business has to check your credentials."

"Nellie, if Harry thinks this is the way you get a job, then you shouldn't try to dissuade him," Ethel said. "Anyway, it's stuffy in the house, and I like the idea of taking a stroll around the square." She turned to Harry. "After you get your job tonight, you can then buy us ice-cream cones."

"That's a deal," Harry said.

When the three of them reached the square, they linked arms, with Harry in the middle, and joined what seemed like half of Independence on the crowded sidewalks.

"Well, if the rest of the people are looking

for jobs, too, Harry, then I think you might be out of luck," Nellie teased him.

"Harry stands out, Nellie," Ethel countered. "It wouldn't matter if there were fifty people applying for the same job, because one look at Harry and the owner of the shop would send the rest of them away."

Just as they passed J. H. Clinton's Drugstore, which stood at the northeast corner of the square, Harry stopped. In the window was a sign that said: HELP WANTED.

"I think I'll apply here," Harry told his cousins. "Of all the drugstores in Independence, my mother likes Mr. Clinton's the best."

Although the drugstore was closed, Harry could see a light at the back. He tapped lightly on the display window. In a few minutes, Mr. Clinton came to the door.

Harry pointed to the HELP WANTED sign, then he pointed to himself.

Mr. Clinton seemed to think about it for a minute, then he unlocked the door and opened it. "It's Harry Truman, isn't it?" Mr. Clinton said.

Harry nodded. "Yes, sir, and these are my cousins Ethel and Nellie Noland."

"Good evening, ladies," Mr. Clinton said. "Well, won't you come in, and we can discuss this."

The three of them stepped inside.

Mr. Clinton closed and locked the front door. "Why don't you sit on the stools at the soda fountain?" he said. "We'll discuss the job over sodas."

As Mr. Clinton made three sodas, he told Harry what the job entailed. "You'll have to come in each weekday and Saturday morning at six thirty. You'll sweep the sidewalk, mop the floor, wipe the counters, and do as much dusting and other cleaning as you have time for until I open for business at seven o'clock. Do you think you can do all of that before you have to leave for school?"

Harry nodded. "Yes, sir, Mr. Clinton," he

said. "I will be here promptly at six thirty Monday morning."

"Good," Mr. Clinton said. He pushed the sodas across the counter to Harry and his cousins. "Now, enjoy!"

When Harry got home that night, he immediately asked everyone to come into the parlor. "I have an important announcement to make," he said. As soon as everyone was seated, Harry told them about his new job.

"I'll be working every morning before I go to school and then all day Saturday."

"Oh, Harry, that's wonderful," Mary Jane said. "I'll come in next Saturday, and you can make me a special milk shake."

"I want a sundae with lots of cherries and nuts," Vivian said.

"Well, I won't be working behind the soda fountain at first," Harry told them, "I'll mostly be sweeping the floors and dusting the bottles."

"That doesn't sound like much fun," Mary Jane said.

"It's a job, Mary Jane," Harry told her. "It's not supposed to be fun."

"Did you say you had to be there at six thirty?" Mrs. Truman said. "How in the world will you get into the store at that time of the morning without waking up Mr. Clinton?" Mr. Clinton lived above the store.

"Mr. Clinton gave me a key to the front door," Harry said. He pulled a big key out of his pocket and showed it to them.

"Oh, Harry, it makes me so nervous to think that you actually have a key to Mr. Clinton's drugstore," Mrs. Truman said. "What if you lose it? What would happen then? After all, it's not only his store that you have to worry about, but it's his home, too."

"Mattie, you of all people shouldn't be thinking that Harry's so irresponsible that he's going to lose that key," Mr. Truman said. "If Mr.

Clinton trusts him, then you should too."

"Oh, John, that's not what I meant. You know I trust Harry," Mrs. Truman said. She turned to Harry. "I just . . ."

"It's all right, Mama. I understand your concern, and you shouldn't think that I'm upset about what you said," Harry told her. "It is a big responsibility, and I have the same concerns that you do. Even if I misplaced the key by accident, it could cause serious problems for Mr. Clinton, so I promised him, and I'm promising you now, that I'll be extra careful with this key."

The following Monday morning, just before six thirty, Harry inserted the big key into the front door of J. H. Clinton's Drugstore, turned it, heard the satisfying click, and let himself into the building, remembering to relock the door after him.

For just a second, he looked around at the darkened interior, suddenly amazed at what was happening. He, Harry S. Truman, was considered trustworthy enough by one of the most important businessmen in Independence to be given a key that would allow him to enter this establishment by himself. On reflection, Harry realized that something like this would not happen to just anyone. It was a matter of building a reputation for honesty day by day. Harry knew that no amount of money in the world could buy this for someone.

Harry took a deep breath and hurried to the storeroom at the back of the drugstore. He got out two big buckets and two big mops to use for scrubbing and rinsing the floor. After just a few minutes of pushing the mop back and forth across the floor, the muscles in his arms were starting to ache, but he didn't let up.

To take his mind off the pain, he tried to picture how he would look with really muscular arms, like the ones he had seen on wrestlers and strongmen in magazine pictures. That helped.

Then he got out two push brooms for sweeping in front of the store. One broom was for the sidewalk, Mr. Clinton had told him, and the other broom was for the gutter.

Harry unlocked the front door and stepped outside into the cool morning air. He started sweeping the sidewalk toward the gutter so he could dump the dust and litter there. After the sidewalk was clean, Harry swept the gutter, and then he put all the dirt and litter into a big metal container.

Just as he started back toward the front door of the drugstore, he noticed Mr. Clinton standing there. Harry was so shocked, he couldn't say anything. He had been working as fast as he could, but he hadn't yet dusted inside, and if it was time for him to go to school, he didn't know what he was going to do.

"Good morning, Harry," Mr. Clinton said. "How are you?"

"I think I'm all right, Mr. Clinton, but I guess I should have been working faster," Harry said. "I haven't finished yet. I can—"

"Oh, you still have time, Harry," Mr. Clinton said. "It's not yet seven o'clock. I just came down early to see how you were doing, and I think you're doing very well."

"Thank you, Mr. Clinton," Harry said. "I've been working steadily since I got here."

"The sidewalk is clean, and the floors are spotless," Mr. Clinton told him. "I'm proud of you." He opened the front door for Harry to come in. "If you don't finish dusting the rest of the store this morning, then you can do it tomorrow."

Harry got a dust cloth and started dusting the counters.

In a few minutes, Mr. Clinton said, "It's almost time for you to leave for school, Harry, but before you do, I want to show you something."

Harry hurried over to where Mr. Clinton

was standing in front of a counter where he kept medicines. "You have to be very careful in handling these bottles, Harry," he said, "because they'll break easily, and it isn't always easy to get some of this medicine."

"Yes, sir," Harry said.

"Why don't you dust here for a few minutes so I can see how you do?" Mr. Clinton said.

As Harry started to wipe the bottles, he thought he recognized Latin words on them. He asked Mr. Clinton about it.

"You're right, Harry, those words are in Latin," Mr. Clinton said. "It's a very important language in medicine."

Harry had just started studying Latin this year in high school. He hoped that when he was further along he'd be able to read most of the words on these bottles.

Morning after morning, all week, Harry arrived at Mr. Clinton's right before six thirty and let himself in. The moping and the rinsing and the sweeping and the dusting got easier and easier. Harry's arm muscles no longer ached. Each morning, as Harry was dusting the bottles of medicine, he would choose one Latin word and then, after he got to school, look it up. Slowly, in addition to a literary vocabulary in Latin, he had also acquired a medical vocabulary.

On Saturday evening, after the drugstore had closed, Mr. Clinton gave Harry three silver dollars. "This is your first week's salary, Harry," he said. "I also have to tell you that you are the best worker I have ever had."

"Thank you, Mr. Clinton," Harry said, "but I know there is always room for improvement, so next week, I'll do even better."

Mr. Clinton shook Harry's hand. "Tomorrow is the Lord's Day, and a day of rest, Harry, but I'll see you bright and early Monday morning."

"Yes, sir, Mr. Clinton," Harry said.

Harry hurried straight home from the drugstore. All week he had been thinking about what he wanted to do with the money he earned.

Harry rushed to the kitchen, where he found his parents sitting at the table.

"We were just having apple pie and coffee," Mrs. Truman said. "Would you like for me to cut you a piece?"

"I'm not hungry, Mama," Harry said. "Mr. Clinton let me have a dish of ice cream before I left." He took the three sliver dollars out of his pocket and laid them on the table in front of his father. "These are for the family, Papa, to help with all of the expenses."

Mr. Truman's hand covered the three dollars, and he moved them back across the table to Harry. "No, son, this money belongs to you," he said. "It's very considerate of you to offer it, but you've worked very hard to earn this money, and your mother and I want you to keep it for your own use."

Mrs. Truman nodded her agreement.

"We're proud of you for working so hard, Harry," she said. "There are always special things that you're wanting, so now you have the money to buy them."

At first, Harry was disappointed, because he had thought all week about how wonderful it would be to help with the family expenses. But at the same time he liked the idea of having his own money so he could buy some things that might not otherwise have fit into the family budget.

As it turned out, Harry only worked at Mr. Clinton's drugstore for a few months.

One night, when Harry had to stay up later than usual studying for a test, his mother said, "Your father and I have been discussing your job at Mr. Clinton's, Harry, and we're both afraid that it's going to start having a negative effect on your grades."

Although Harry didn't show it, his initial

reaction to his mother's comment was anger, but that lasted only for a few seconds, because he knew she was right.

"You've always been such a fine student," Mrs. Truman continued, "and your father and I don't want anything interfering with your getting a good education."

"You're right, Mama. I've actually been thinking the same thing," Harry said. "I just didn't want you and Papa to think I was a quitter."

"Oh, Harry," Mrs. Truman said, giving him a hug, "your father and I would never think that about you."

The next morning, Harry gave Mr. Clinton his two weeks' notice. Mr. Clinton was disappointed, but he fully understood Harry's reason.

"Just remember, though, Harry," he said. "If you ever need your job back, I'll give it to you in a minute, and if you ever need a recommendation for another job, I'll give that to you, too, because I've never had a young man who's worked as hard as you have."

"Thank you, Mr. Clinton," Harry said. "I appreciate that very much."

After Harry quit his job at the drugstore, Ethel invited him to start studying at her house on Saturday afternoons.

"It was actually Mama and Nellie's idea to invite our friends over," she told him. "We all gather around the big dining room table so we can spread out our books and notebooks."

"That sounds like a great idea," Harry said. "That way, we can discuss any problems we had in a particular subject the past week."

"Exactly," Ethel said.

"Who all comes?" Harry inquired.

"Oh, lots of people," Ethel said. She named several of her and Harry's classmates. When she saw the disappointment on Harry's face, she said, "Oh, yes, I almost forgot. From time to time, Bess Wallace comes too!"

Harry grinned. "I'm positive that I'm going to have a lot of questions to ask Bess," he said.

Graduation Day

It was Friday afternoon, and Harry was walking up the steps of the Independence Public Library. Most of the rest of his friends and classmates were headed downtown to plan their weekend activities over a soda, but Harry had some reading he wanted to do.

As Harry opened the front door and went inside, Miss Wallace called out, "Is that you, Harry?"

"Yes, ma'am," Harry said.

Normally, Miss Wallace's voice would have been more muted, but Harry knew that most of the day's patrons would be gone by now, and since it was a Friday afternoon, no other high school students would be there. Even Charlie Ross, who along with Harry had vowed to read all of the two thousand volumes housed here, including encyclopedias, had family matters to take care of.

Harry made his way to the "parlor," where Miss Wallace had tea waiting for him.

"Earl Grey today?" Miss Wallace said, the teapot suspended in midair over a teacup.

"That sounds wonderful," Harry said.

Miss Wallace poured Harry's cup of tea, put in two lumps of sugar, then stirred in a little cream and handed it to him. "How was school today?" she asked.

"Sometimes I feel like a bottomless pitcher, and I don't really understand it, Miss Wallace," Harry said. He took a sip of tea. "The teachers just keep pouring more and more information into me, and I never get filled up."

"Well, Harry, that is an interesting metaphor," Miss Wallace said. "I wish more young people felt that way, but I'm afraid they often can't wait to empty the pitcher of what they learned in school and replace it with meaningless trivia."

While Harry finished his tea, Miss Wallace told him about the new books she had received that day. "I've put them on our special shelf," she said, giving him a conspiratorial grin, "and you know it's the last shelf I show anyone else."

Harry and Miss Wallace had had this discussion before. Since this was a public library, she had to put the books out for all of the patrons, but she made sure that any book she thought Harry would want to read was somehow not available to anyone else until he had read it first.

Miss Wallace stood up. "I'll leave you to your reading, Harry," she said. "I have some administrative details to take care of now."

There was a small reading table by a window at the back of the stacks, which Harry considered his private domain. It was hidden, so he could read and think without being disturbed.

History was a passion for Harry. It was difficult for him to explain to other people, but he needed to read about what famous men did in their lives. He had worked his way through several shelves of books on ancient Egypt, Greece, and Rome.

At home, reading the books that his parents had bought, he had already learned about Andrew Jackson, Hannibal, and Robert E. Lee. Now to that list he added Cincinnatus, Scipio, Cyrus the Great, and Gustav Adolph III, the seventeenth-century Swedish king. He was drawn to the lives of great generals. In fact, at times, he thought that he himself wanted a career in the military.

After Harry got home that evening, he ate dinner with his family, and then he went into the parlor to study Latin. He had already mastered most of the intricacies of the grammar, so his teacher, Miss Hardin, had given him several of her own books for him to start reading. He was in the middle of a Roman military campaign when Mary Jane, with two of her friends, asked if he could go somewhere else so that one of the girls could play the piano.

Dutifully, Harry picked up his books and headed into the kitchen.

"Well, Harry, I see you're being moved from pillar to post," Aunt Caroline said, "but if you want to sit in here and read, I'll make sure you're not disturbed."

"Thank you, Aunt Caroline," Harry said. He pulled out a chair and sat down at the kitchen table. "I guess I should be doing something else tonight, but there is just so much to learn that if I'm not reading, I feel as though I'm wasting my time."

"That's the way some of us are, Harry, and other people just don't often understand us,"

Aunt Caroline said, "but we always have to be true to ourselves, and we can't worry about what people think we should be doing."

Aunt Caroline went back to her baking so that Harry could return to his reading, but as quite often happened, Harry was left to ponder her words of wisdom, which were just as meaningful as anything he read.

A lot of his classmates seemed quite content to read the poorly written novels that you could pick up in town, but Harry wanted the classics. His English teacher, Miss Matilda Brown, had made James Fenimore Cooper and William Shakespeare come alive for him. After he had translated ten pages of Latin, he finished an essay he was writing on *The Last of the Mohicans*, and then, as it was near midnight, he decided that he'd go to bed. Tomorrow he'd finish the rest of the reading and writing he needed to do before Monday.

* * * *

There was only one thing that would keep Harry from reading or writing, and that was the piano.

The next day, Saturday, Harry had just started the first act of *The Merchant of Venice* when his mother knocked on his door.

"Come in," Harry said.

His mother had a big smile on her face. "As you can see, I'm dressed for visiting, and your father has the buggy ready downstairs," she said, "so if you'll hurry up and get dressed, you and I are going into Kansas City."

Harry stood up. "And what is the purpose of this visit, may I ask?" he said. He loved to play these little games with his mother.

"I had a long talk with Miss Burrus last night," Mrs. Truman said. "She told us that she has taught you everything she knows about the piano."

"She's a very good teacher, and I enjoy playing for her," Harry said. "I'm sure I haven't learned everything."

"Well, Miss Burrus feels that you have, so she talked to Mrs. E. C. White in Kansas City about taking you as a pupil," Mrs. Truman said. "Mrs. White has agreed to do that, and your lessons start this morning."

Harry was dumbfounded. He was well aware that Mrs. White had studied under Fannie Bloomfield Zeisler, one of the leading pianists in America, as well as with Theodor Leschetizky, who had been one of Ignacy Paderewski's teachers.

Harry could not believe his good fortune. "I'll be ready in five minutes!" he said excitedly.

Harry and Mrs. White liked each other right away. She opened new worlds for him, and to please her, Harry started practicing two hours each day, without fail, starting at five o'clock in the morning. After just a few weeks of studying with Mrs. White, Harry thought he had the makings of a concert pianist, and so did Mrs. White.

Now Harry had even less time for his friends. As they headed downtown to see what fun they could have, Harry was boarding the streetcar to Kansas City. While Harry often took good-natured kidding from them, because he always seemed to have rolled up sheets of music under his arms, there was never anything mean-spirited about it. To the rest of the young people in Independence, Harry was just Harry, and that's all there was to it. They might not be interested in doing what he was doing, but they accepted the fact that this was what interested him most: long hours reading in the library, and long hours playing the piano. He was admired for his fortitude.

One day when Harry arrived at Mrs. White's house on Brooklyn Street in Kansas City, his first question was, "Which composer's music am I supposed to master today?"

Mrs. White gave him a big smile and replied, "Mendelssohn's 'Songs without Words.'"

Over the next few weeks, Mrs. White would also drill him in Bach, Beethoven, and Grieg. He especially liked the new "Woodland Sketches" by the American composer Edward MacDowell.

He mastered Paderewski's Minuet in G, and several Chopin waltzes.

"I love sad music," Harry told Mrs. White one afternoon, so she gave him Beethoven's Sonata in C Minor—"Pathétique" and Chopin's "Funeral March."

But of all the composers Mrs. White introduced Harry to, he preferred Chopin.

"I want to learn the Ninth Sonata," Harry told Mrs. White.

"That's the secret of learning anything, Harry," Mrs. White said. "*Wanting* to do it."

With Mrs. White's help, Harry mastered the piece.

At home, much to Vivian's chagrin, Harry was now playing mostly serious classical music. Now, too, instead of going to parties, he went to concerts at every opportunity.

Twice, when Fannie Bloomfield Zeisler performed at the Lyceum in Kansas City, Harry was in the audience, a guest of Mrs. White. They listened to her play Scarlatti's "Pastorale" and "Capriccio" and Beethoven's Sonata, op. 111.

Mrs. White also took him to hear Paderewski and arranged for a meeting backstage with the great pianist. Harry was even treated to a private demonstration of how to play his "Minuet in G."

At home, life had begun to change in subtle ways. Harry's father seemed to have mellowed in his relationship with him.

"You have a lot of ability, Harry," Mr. Truman told him one day. "I like the way you never have an idle moment."

Of course, Harry attributed part of this new relationship to the fact that Vivian had now developed into a sturdy man who was good at games and wasn't interested in books or piano lessons. Vivian was interested in all the same things their father was interested in and, because of that, Harry was left to go his own way.

For instance, Vivian had already shown that he could trade horses as well as any man in Jackson County. Mr. Truman gave him a checkbook and set him up as a partner. Harry had neither the interest nor the ability in this kind of business.

There was nothing about Vivian's new relationship with their father that angered Harry, though. He and his brother remained close, and Harry held no grudges.

Although Harry had no business acumen, he did share with his father an abiding love of politics.

In the summer of 1900, Harry accompanied his father to Kansas City to attend the Democratic National Convention. When they arrived, Mr. Truman said, "I have a surprise for you, Harry. Mr. Kemper has asked me to sit with him in his box. I told him that you'd be available to run errands for him."

Now Harry was even more excited. William T. Kemper was one of his father's friends in the grain business and one of Kansas City's most prominent citizens. He was also a Democratic Party national committeeman, which meant he'd have a say in who was to be the Democratic Party's next candidate for president of the United States.

For the next few days, Harry threw himself into the world of politics. He made sure that each request made of him by Mr. Kemper was taken care of immediately. He enjoyed himself immensely and was rewarded with constant praise.

Harry had never in his life seen so many people in one place. In all, seventeen thousand people from all over the United States were in Kansas City for the convention.

Finally, William Jennings Bryan was chosen to run against William McKinley. The nominating speech touched off a demonstration that lasted for half an hour.

Harry hated to see the convention end. On the ride back to Independence, he tried to solve a dilemma he was having: How could he possibly choose among a life in music, a life in the military, or a life in politics? He liked all three equally.

At three P.M. on May 30, 1901, the senior class of Independence High School gathered in front of the school's main entrance for the class picture.

"Stand where you like," the photographer told them, "and if I see a problem with the composition, I'll move some of you around."

The members of the class began positioning themselves on the steps, chatting amiably with one another as they decided who would go where and who would stand next to whom.

No one said anything to Harry as he slowly and unobtrusively made his way to the back row. He stood there by himself. Bess was at the far end of the second row. Harry was about as far away from her as he could be.

While the photographer made a few minor adjustments, Harry's mind was on his preparations to take the examination to enter West Point. Even though Harry had never in his life been in a fight and was admittedly afraid of guns, he thought he would make a very good general. Or, he added to himself, a concert pianist or a politician.

That night, it seemed to Harry that half of Independence was packed into the high school auditorium.

Before his parents and Vivian and Mary Jane took their seats, Mrs. Truman made some last-minute adjustments to the stiff collar Harry was wearing with his dark suit.

"There!" Mrs. Truman said. "You look quite distinguished."

"Thanks, Mama," Harry said.

"Smile when they give you your diploma, Harry," Mary Jane said. "You've been looking too serious lately."

Harry quickly practiced giving her a big smile. "How about that?" he asked.

"That's good," Mary Jane said.

"If we don't hurry, we won't get good seats," Mr. Truman told them. He shook hands with Harry. "We're proud of you, son," he added.

"Thanks, Papa," Harry said.

Vivian shook hands with him, too, and slapped him on the back.

Just then, Miss Burrus played a piano chord, which was the signal for everyone to line up.

As the members of the Senior Class of 1901 marched into the auditorium, the girls in white dresses, the boys in their dark suits, Harry looked out into the audience and saw family and friends. It was hard for him to believe that this moment in his life had come and in an hour or so would be gone. He was seventeen years old. His childhood was over. Tomorrow, he would begin a new chapter in his life. He felt ready to deal with whatever was handed him.

From the Farm to Washington, D.C.

West Point turned Harry down because of his poor eyesight, so while he now had no definite plans for the future, he still had determination and the willingness to work. Harry Truman had never felt that the world owed him a living.

In the first few years after Harry graduated from high school, he held several different kinds of jobs in order to making a living. Because he had always been interested in trains, he became a timekeeper for a construction gang on the Sante Fe Railroad. After that, he worked for a few weeks wrapping newspapers in the mail room of the *Kansas City Star.* Through a friend, he learned of an opening for a bookkeeper at the National Bank of Commerce. He got the job. Later, he took his newly learned bookkeeping skills to the Union National Bank, which had agreed to pay him a little more money.

With his weekends free, Harry got a second job as an usher at the Grand Theater in Kansas City. It was during this time that he joined the Missouri National Guard, and he regularly attended practice sessions.

Two years later, after Vivian had graduated from high school, financial disaster struck the Truman family. John Truman sold their home in Independence, and he and Mrs. Truman and Mary Jane moved back to Grandma Young's farm so that Mr. Truman could take over the job of managing it. Harry and Vivian moved to a boardinghouse in Kansas City.

In 1906, Harry's life changed once again. He moved back to Grandma Young's farm to help his father take care of it. It wasn't long before Mr. Truman decided to let Harry take over as manager. Harry had never forgotten how to do farmwork, and he remained on the farm for ten successful years.

During this time, Harry did whatever needed to be done, often working from long before sunrise until long after sunset. He still had time to participate in local politics, though, and soon was regarded as an important community leader.

Being on the farm didn't keep Harry from making frequent visits to Kansas City, or to Independence, either—he often went there to visit family and friends, especially Bess Wallace. His visits to her began to take on a regularity. As these visits increased, Harry purchased a secondhand automobile, mainly to make it easier to visit Bess.

The years on the farm were not always happy, though. In 1909, Grandma Young died. In 1914, Harry's father died following an injury.

The United States entered World War I in the spring of 1917. As a member of the Missouri National Guard, Harry immediately went into the Army and helped organize a field artillery regiment. It wasn't long before he was commissioned a lieutenant.

In early 1918, Harry was sent to France. Shortly after his arrival, he was promoted to captain. He was frequently involved in fierce combat. On November 11, 1918, the fighting stopped, and the war was finally over. Harry stayed in Europe for several months, where he was involved in postwar duties. In May 1919, he returned to the United States, where he was discharged with the rank of major.

All during this time, Harry and Bess had been writing to each other. About eight weeks after Harry returned, they were married in the Trinity Episcopal Church in Independence. They moved into the big frame house on North Delaware Street. Even during the time the Trumans were in

Washington, D.C., living in the White House, they would always consider this their home.

Harry decided to start a men's clothing store in Kansas City. He put in long hours, hoping to make the business a success, but unfortunately it failed. It was a bitter disappointment to him. For the first time in his life, Harry Truman began to think that he was a failure.

Neither Bess nor political friends of Harry's from years past would let this happen, though, and when he ran for the position of district judge of Jackson County in 1922, he won. His job was to help manage the business affairs of the county. During this time, in 1924, the Trumans' daughter, Margaret, was born.

Harry proved to be a very efficient and popular judge. In 1926, he was elected presiding judge of Jackson County. Once again, he proved to be so successful that he was reelected to the same office four years later.

In 1934, Harry was nominated as the Democratic candidate for the United States Senate. He easily won the election. He was now ready to represent Missouri in Washington, D.C.

As a senator, Harry gained a reputation for being dependable. The voters of Missouri liked and trusted him, so in 1940, he was elected to a second term.

In 1939, when World War II started in Europe, the United States started spending a lot of money for military equipment and supplies, such as ammunition, airplanes, and warships, and for the training of soldiers, to make sure that the country was prepared in case it had to enter the conflict.

As a senator, part of Harry's job was to make sure the money for these projects was spent wisely. It didn't take him long to notice that a lot of it was being wasted. He immediately began an investigation and found that a lot of people were cheating the government.

All throughout his years as a senator, Harry Truman was admired by many people, including President Franklin D. Roosevelt. In the summer of 1944, when the Democratic Convention nominated President Roosevelt for a fourth term in office, he chose Harry as his vice-presidential candidate. In the election that fall, they won by an overwhelming margin.

President Roosevelt was inaugurated for his fourth term as president on January 20, 1945. Harry was inaugurated as vice president.

On April 12, 1945, just a few months later, President Roosevelt died in Warm Springs, Georgia, where he had gone for a much-needed rest. Harry S. Truman was now the president of the United States.

President Truman

Harry was in shock.

Nothing had really prepared him for this moment. Although President Roosevelt liked him, he had never actually included Harry in most of the meetings where important decisions were made. Harry knew that in his first few months as president he would be spending a lot of long hours in the White House learning the job. Still, he was ready to take on the task. He knew that the people of the United States had confidence in him.

The United States was still involved in World

War II, both in Europe and in the Pacific. Fortunately for President Truman, though, the war in Europe was almost over, which meant that he could concentrate most of his time on finding ways to end the hostilities with Japan.

On April 25, 1945, there was a meeting of world leaders in San Francisco to set up an organization to maintain peace in the world after the war was over. Most of the leaders stopped in Washington, D.C., on their way to San Francisco, where they received an official greeting from President Truman.

Less than two weeks after this meeting, on May 8, 1945, Germany surrendered, and the war in Europe was over. President Truman announced the news by radio to the American people. He reminded everyone, however, that the job was only half done. The war in the Pacific was still raging.

On June 26, 1945, President Truman flew to San Francisco to witness the signing of the United Nations Charter.

The spring and summer of 1945 was a busy time for President Truman. In July, he flew to Potsdam, Germany, to meet with Prime Minister Winston Churchill of Great Britain and Premier Joseph Stalin of the Soviet Union. The three men discussed ways to rebuild Europe. They also urged Japan to surrender.

The United States had a secret weapon it had been working on for years. It was called the atomic bomb.

When Japan refused to surrender, President Truman sent a single airplane to drop the bomb on Hiroshima. Almost the entire city was destroyed. When Japan still refused to surrender, President Truman ordered another bomb dropped on Nagasaki. That brought an end to the war.

The Japanese government officially surrendered on September 2, 1945. The ceremony took place in Tokyo Bay aboard the USS *Missouri*. The ship, named after President

Truman's home state, had been christened by his daughter, Margaret.

Now that the war was over, President Truman turned to the problems in the United States. He asked Congress to pass the G.I. Bill of Rights. This would give returning soldiers money until they could find a job. President Truman also had to work hard to keep prices and wages from rising too quickly so they wouldn't affect the postwar economy.

Even though World War II was over, there were still problems in the world that needed to be solved. President Truman was worried that the Soviet Union wanted to set up Communist governments in Greece and Turkey. He came up with a plan called the Truman Doctrine to keep this from happening. The United States gave Greece and Turkey a lot of money to help them rebuild their countries. To keep the Soviet Union from taking over other countries in Europe, President Truman established a similar program for them. It was called the Marshall Plan, after Secretary of State George C. Marshall.

When the Soviet Union blocked the highway leading from West Germany to Berlin, President Truman began the Berlin Airlift. Planes flew in food, fuel, medicine, and other necessary supplies to the people of that city. Several months later, the Soviet Union reopened the highway.

In early 1948, President Truman encouraged the United Nations to establish a new country for the Jews of the world. Soon thereafter, Israel was formed, and the United States was the first nation to recognize it as a sovereign state.

Later that summer, the Democratic National Convention nominated President Truman as its candidate to run against Thomas E. Dewey, governor of New York, who was the Republican National Convention candidate. Everyone thought that Governor Dewey would win. In fact, one newspaper even carried the headline *Dewey Defeats Truman*. But President Truman won the election.

In the spring of 1949, representatives from the United States, Canada, and several countries in Europe met in Washington, D.C., to form NATO, the North Atlantic Treaty Organization. These countries decided that if any one of them were attacked by the Soviet Union, they would all fight together.

In 1950, North Korea, a Communist government, invaded South Korea. President Truman sent in American troops, under the command of General Douglas MacArthur, to help protect South Korea. But when General MacArthur wanted to invade China, President Truman objected. When General MacArthur complained, President Truman fired him.

While President Truman was dealing with foreign affairs, he also had to handle serious domestic problems, such as strikes by coal miners and railroad and steel workers. He also encouraged Congress to amend the United

States Constitution so that a President could not serve more than two four-year terms. Because President Truman had actually only been elected by the people of the United States to one term, he could have run again, but he declined.

The Trumans left Washington, D.C., on January 20, 1953, and moved back to their home on North Delaware Street in Independence. Three years later, their daughter, Margaret, married Elbert Clifton Daniel Jr., a prominent journalist with the *New York Times*. They made their home in New York City, although they would often visit Independence.

Over the next few years, President Truman read a lot of books, wrote his memoirs, and carried on an extensive correspondence with friends and family. He also took lots of walks around his neighborhood and oversaw the construction of the Truman Library in Independence.

Gradually, President Truman's health declined. He died on December 26, 1972, in a Kansas City hospital. He was eighty-eight years old.

President Truman's beloved wife, Bess, died on October 18, 1982. She and President Truman are buried next to each other in the courtyard of the Truman Library.

For More Information

BOOKS

Byrnes, Mark S.
The Truman Years: 1945-1953.
London: Longman, 2000.

Ferrell, Robert H.
Harry S. Truman: A Life.
Columbia: University of Missouri Press, 1994.

Ferrell, Robert H.
Harry S. Truman: His Life on the Family Farms.
Worland, Wyoming: High Plains, 1991.

Hamby, Alonzo L.
Man of the People: A Life of Harry S. Truman.
New York: Oxford University Press, 1995.

McCullough, David.
Truman.
New York: Simon & Schuster, 1992.

Paterson, Thomas G., ed.
The Origins of the Cold War, Second Edition.
Lexington, Massachusetts: D. C. Heath, 1974.

Truman, Harry S.
Memoirs, Volume One: Year of Decisions.
Garden City, New York: Doubleday &
 Company, Inc., 1955.

Truman, Harry S.
*Memoirs, Volume Two: Years of Trial
 and Hope.*
Garden City, New York: Doubleday &
 Company, Inc., 1956.

Schuman, Michael A.
Harry S. Truman.
Berkeley Heights, New Jersey: Enslow
  Publishers, Inc., 1997.

Stone, I. F.
The Truman Era.
New York: Random House, 1953.

VIDEO

Truman.
HBO Original Movies.
Gary Sinise, Diana Scarwid, and Richard
  Dysart. Frank Pierson, Dir. 1995.

WEB SITES

www.ci.independence.mo.us

www.nps.gov/hstr

www.trumanlibrary.org